ABOUT

"WOMEN ON TOP: A DUD'S TALE"

In a utopian near future, women run the world, and they have finally sorted it out.

Nurturing the earth back to health following centuries of male violence, and creating a pristine commercial paradise, women have separated men into those that are fertile, Studs, and those that are useless, Duds.

It is one such Dud, he who is labelled Wimpole, who threatens this paradise. Mistakenly assigned as a Stud through a (male) clerical error, and assigned to impregnate the noble Commandress Roseanne, Dud Wimpole threatens the very fabric of our ideal future society.

It is the account of Dud Wimpole that is presented here, in full, discovered by a present day Primary school teacher, highlighting the dangers of allowing men to read and write, and reminding us all why they should not be allowed anywhere near Primary schools.

The text is offered as part of collection in this volume, with a modern adaptation for the internet of Louisa May Alcott's towering work of art, Little Women, and a short piece of realist fiction examining marital relationships.

WOMEN ON TOP

Women on Top

Daniel Silman & Sean Freeman

A NOTE ABOUT THE FONT

You will, no doubt, have noticed that this text uses the EB Garamond font in size 12. The EB Garamond font, designed by Earnest Bellomew Garamond in 1932, is a bold, masculine font with pronounced curvature and rich flavours. The font is noted for its functional, shortened cross-lines on the 'ts" and "hs," cementing its reputation as perhaps the most masculine of all fonts. It was this masculinity which Garamond's wife objected to, when she divorced him in 1935, and tried to claim the font as her own. She had, in the years leading to the divorce, told all her friends, and those of her husband, that it was she who had designed the font, and that her husband had taken it for himself, shortening the through lines, heightening the font's masculinity, and ruining the font entirely. EB Garamond countered with the observation that it would be unlikely for his former wife to be the creator of the font, since she had never designed a font, before, nor had she ever shown any interest in designing fonts, and that he, as the professional font designer in the family, was obviously the originator. By then it was too late. The former Mrs. Garamond had spent so much of the preceding years telling anyone who would listen that she had created the EB Garamond font, that the thing became a received fact. EB Garamond lamented on his death bed a few short years later that not only had his wife taken his house, his furniture and his book collection, she had also taken his favourite font. The font is used here in his memory.

CONTENTS

A Dud's Tale

"When I was in nursery school, the teachers asked me, y' know, 'What does your dad do for a living?' So I said 'He helps women get pregnant.'" Natalie Portman

ITEM 1: NEWSPAPER CUTTING FROM THANET GAZETTE - BY CINDY STERLING

Local school children uncover notes from the future in school time capsule

Local news: Children at Garlinge School in Thanet were surprised to find handwritten notes seemingly written in the future.

The Year 3 children found the pages, dated 2050, and titled "A Dud's Tale," when unpacking the contents from a time capsule buried on school grounds in 1950.

Amid items clearly dated from the 1950s, including a tin of spam, postcards from the post-war period, and faded drawings from Garlinge School children, were these strange, handwritten pages, inscribed on translucent, plastic sheets, and signed by one "Dud Wimpole."

Having shielded the children from the contents of the pages, Headmistress June Spencer has advised they seem to have been written by "a pervert."

The teacher who uncovered the pages with the class, and placing the impressionable minds at risk of their contents, one Mr. Bellington, has been suspended subject to an inquest.

ITEM 2: EXPLANATION REGARDING "A DUD'S TALE," – BY FRED BELLINGTON

When I brought my Year 3 class down to the school allotment to uncover the time capsule, buried there in 1950, I was expecting to find some interesting remnants of the past that would be of use to introduce the children to social history.

I was as surprised as anyone to find the futuristic looking "paper," wrapped in a plastic envelope, dated 2050, and labelled "A Dud's Tale." At first I assumed it was some joke, perhaps placed there in recent times by some errant graduate. Clearly the pages were too "new" to have been there since the 1950s.

The kids asked me to read to them what was written, but when I noticed the first chapter was called "The Gonad Assessment Centre," I realised that what was presented was not intended for the eyes of the young, and a quick scan of the pages on the way back to class gave me the impression that the text was in fact written by some sort of weirdo.

Before handing the pages over to our Headmistress, Ms. Hendricks, I read the account in full, rushing through the pages on my lunch break, photographing each one for my records, and then handing them in over her desk that afternoon.

Ms. Hendricks read the thing herself and promptly suspended me without pay.

As the only male teacher in the school, I've often been looked towards with suspicion. "What's he doing here?" I'd hear the other teachers whisper behind my back. "Don't you find him a bit odd?" I'd endure the dinner ladies saying to one another, right in front of me, after they'd served me mashed potatoes. This "Dud's Tale" business seemed to confirm their suspicions.

The suspension gave me time to ponder.

Certainly, the whole thing could have been a joke, but for what purpose?

There was something about the narrative, however, some urgency in the writing perhaps, that gave me reason to doubt that a jest was not the intention of the author.

What if, I found myself asking, time was relative, as Einstein had said, and time capsules not only saved items from the past but also, somehow, collected items from the future? These were the thoughts that entered my mind as I immediately turned to drink after my suspension, and rapidly began my decline.

There were questions about the account which I could not resolve, inconsistencies, anachronisms. How had certain items in the culture filtered into the future with others seemingly lost or forgotten about? How could such a society, as depicted in the account, one that was so one-sided, be created unopposed? How could any of it be anything other than the imaginings of an absurd imbecile?

I found myself, however, thinking about the author from time to time, the one they labelled "Dud Wimpole." I thought of him when being pushed in front of by a procession of grannies when queuing for a bus. I thought of him when passing by a McDonalds, where a group of teenage girls shouted at me, "Oi, Harry Potter, where you's goin'?" I thought of him when the tribunal of Headteachers and Primary assistants concluded that they would not feel comfortable allowing me back on school grounds, considering my "attempted subversions," and recommended that I not only be removed from my position but that I "be put on some kind of register, somewhere."

And I thought of him when they opened up a "Gonad Assessment Centre," on the edge of town, last week - a fertility centre. A coincidence, perhaps, in that the name appears in the account by Dud Wimpole, but still...

I thought about him then.

I think about him, now.

That's why I present the pages to you. So you can think about him, too...

Fred Bellington
Former Primary School Teacher
10/11/2020

ITEM 3: A DUD'S TALE - TEXT PRESENTED AS FOUND:

PART ONE

PEACE

CHAPTER ONE

THE GONAD ASSESSMENT CENTRE

If you've ever worn one of those hospital gowns with the hole at the back which exposes your buttocks, you'll know what I'm talking about. Except that with the gown I was wearing, the hole was at the front, exposing my penis.

And to make matters worse, this gown had been designed for a much larger man. Not larger in the penis, but larger than 5 foot 5. That said, penises may be proportional to height, but either way, the gown was too big.

I wish I hadn't started this by drawing attention to my penis. It's just that, I'm nervous. This story isn't really about my penis. Well, in a way it is, but...

I'll start again.

It was a cold, windy day. It was overcast, in a way that was ominous, in a literary kind of way. As I and the other testees lined up outside the Gonad Assessment Centre, chained at the ankle, a gust of wind blew across the tarmac and lifted up my gown, exposing my penis.

The guard, a large man with a taser gun, ushered us towards a large iron door, where we stood, awaiting our fate.

I adjusted my glasses and began to whistle.

*

And as often happens whenever I whistle, I found myself having to explain myself.

"How can you be whistling at a time like this?" asked the guy standing in line behind me.

Truth is, I often whistle when I'm nervous. However, mixed with the nerves that remain a permanence in my body, at that time, was a strain of care-free relief.

"Why wouldn't I be whistling," I asked, turning to face the guy.

"What if you're found to be infertile? What if you're a Dud?"

"Of course I'll be found to be infertile. Of course I'm a Dud," I told the guy, proudly.

This whole thing was a waste of time.

Fertility rates had been dropping naturally in males for the past 50 years. Some said it was the result of men living in an increasingly women led society. But the women said it was because we were assholes. The fallout from the nuclear war made things worse.

Now, one in a thousand guys were fertile, and this little visit to the Gonad Assessment Centre was aimed at finding that one in a thousand.

I lived life content in the knowledge that all signs pointed to me being infertile: frail shoulders, hunched back, the inability to play sports, dance or hold a rhythm, a seemingly natural ability to displease and irritate women - without even trying.

I would never get dragged into the whole dangerous business of wooing a female so that I could help her produce clones of herself. I would live my life always trying to avoid as much harm as possible, always taking the easiest of all options, always trying to live pain free.

"You'll be sent to the colonies," wailed the guy, demonstrating wildly with his arms in the air and neglecting to cover his testicles.

That one in a thousand guy would be assigned to the household of a Commandress, to live under her total control, service her every need and attempt to fertilize her eggs. The rest of us would be given a broom, shipped off to the colonies and ordered to sweep nuclear waste until our internal organs disintegrated or our eyeballs exploded from the toxicity of the conditions, usually within three to six months. We were the lucky ones.

"There are far worse things in life than having to sweep nuclear waste all day," I said to the guy, trying to offer some reassurance, but this reassurance was short lived as the huge iron door behind which we lined, was opened.

*

We were ushered into what must have been a converted cow shed. Except that instead of cows standing side by side, waiting in blissful ignorance to be shot in the head, my fellow testees were standing side by side, masturbating into swill buckets. This took me by surprise.

"Excuse me," I said to the rotund Uncle who ushered us into the testing centre. "I thought the assessment would comprise a questionnaire. Isn't there a survey I should fill in?"

Uncles were assigned to deal with the messy business of managing males. This one, identifying himself as Uncle Joe, had seemingly won favour with Commandresses by growing an enormous moustache. He collected us from the arena at the morning ritual, led us to the Gonad Assessment Centre and ushered us inside. Despite being under strict orders to not engage with us under any circumstances, he was very polite.

"Shut up," said Uncle Joe.

Uncle Joe gave me a helpful shove in the back, almost knocking my glasses clean off my face. I took my position in a designated cubicle, at the front of which was carved a waist high partition and on the other side, a swill bucket.

To my left, a fellow testee was working up a sweat, blowing puffs of air through his cheeks, trying in vain to produce a sample. I recognised him as Bob from accounts - that is, the accountant formerly known as Bob, before we were rounded up, our jobs taken, our names removed, before the assignment of uniform gowns and swill buckets.

"Hello, there," said Bob from accounts.

Prior to the round up, men had been permitted to work in largely female serving administrative functions - The Department of Endless Compliments, The Office of Shoe Organisation, The District of Buying Presents...

I'd had a comfortable job of Photoshopping models online to make them look fat. Bob was based down the hall, calculating daily reductions in male salaries to create something called a Totally Natural Gender Pay-Gap.

"Hello," I returned. "How are you?"

"Whacking off into a swill bucket," said the testee formerly known as Bob from accounts.

"Ah, yes, me too," I said, trying to offer some camaraderie. Except that I was doing nothing into a swill bucket, whacking off or otherwise. Not only was I undoubtedly infertile, I was, for as long as I could remember, impotent.

I mean, I recall in my early teens, having shown interest in a girl in school, a sweet teen with pigtails who sat right in front of me.

School, for as long as I had experienced it, had been an ongoing explanation of why boys were wicked and why girls were delightful. Nonetheless, charged by raging teen hormones, I felt emboldened enough one day to pick up the pencil of the delightful pigtailed girl after she had dropped it to the floor.

I rose and stood by her desk, presenting the pencil to her like a knight, returning from a quest in one of those forbidden books that were increasingly being hidden from circulation. Feelings approaching gallantry, chivalry and pride were being awoken in me for the first time. I was a provider, a hero, a man.... She took the pencil, and shoved it up my nose.

From that day on, that little girl ordered me to stand by her desk, while she inserted pencils, pens and staplers into my orifices. I became her human pencil case.

Not wanting to quell the girl's clearly adopted understanding of the school's indoctrination, nor to miss out on a piece of the action, our teacher, who I'd also toyed with having the hots for, began using me as a stand for her coffee cups.

I'd stand there each day, stationary sticking out of my nose, ears and mouth, hot coffee dripping onto my head, and I felt my libido slowly slipping away, never to return.

"Excuse me," I called to Uncle Joe. "I'd like to declare myself as infertile. Where can I collect my broom?"

"You'll do as you're told," growled Uncle Joe.

My situation wasn't helped by the guy on my right, a giant of a man, seemingly in his element.

He too called to Uncle Joe:

"Get hold of the end of mine will you? I can't reach this far! Ha ha ha!"

I fumbled my limp privates out from the gown and rested them onto the partition over the swill bucket. They lay there like the unused pack of giblets that they were. It was no use.

"I can't do it," I protested. "I can't perform under pressure. I can't even perform with pressure."

Uncle Joe returned, looking flustered. I was getting through.

"Watch the erotic stimulant material provided to us by our fair Commandresses," said Uncle Joe, pulling a screen down in front of my head, presumably attached to the guns formerly used to blast the brains out of those lucky cows.

A Department of Communications logo appeared on screen, followed by footage of elderly women, all well into their hundreds, frolicking in malls, trying on make-up, spilling out into the streets carrying hordes of shopping bags and laughing triumphantly to the sky.

Then came the images of them shaving their legs, applying perfume in slow motion, licking their lips to camera…

"What is this?" I asked. "How is this supposed to help?"

"We don't need a trouble maker!" said Uncle Joe, seemingly panicked.

"I'm gonna need a bigger bucket," said the giant to the right.

To my left, Bob from accounts was in tears.

"Look, I didn't want to say this," I protested. "But this is downright demeaning."

Uncle Joe hovered nervously in front of me.

"I can't do this," I exclaimed. "I can't do it and I won't do it."

Uncle Joe took my testicles in his hand and squeezed the contents into the bucket.

"That did it," I said, and I passed out.

CHAPTER TWO

IN THE COMPANY OF MEN

I awoke to a cacophony of farts. The holding quarters for testees, where we waited overnight for the results from our samples, appeared to be a converted basketball court. A faded banner, hanging behind a disused net at the far end, read "No ball games." Another, at the opposite end, read "Sports subvert."

In the darkness, rows of single, fold out beds lined the floor, wall to wall, each occupied by a testee. Our possessions, in my case no more than a rucksack full of hastily gathered items from my apartment, had been placed at the foot of each bed. Uncles patrolled the lines between rows, arms behind their backs, moustaches under their noses…

The testee to my right turned onto his side, and tried to attract the attention of the testee on my left.

"Hey," he whispered. "Hey," and again, "Hey."

"Yeah?" the testee on my left whispered back.

"Psss psss psss psss psss," whispered the testee on my right.

"Huh?" asked the testee on my left.

It was going to be a long night.

"Ah, sssp psss psss. Sssp, sssp, sssp?" offered the testee on the right, rising in intonation at the end, seemingly with a question.

"Oh!" whispered the testee on my left, returning with, "I - psss, psss, sssp, ssssp, pss, pss!"

"Stop whispering, you twerps," said the Uncle, as he passed our beds, twirling his handlebar moustache with a finger. "This ain't a summer camp. Talk normally if you've got something to say."

He stood peering down at me at the head of the bed, as though waiting for an answer.

I tried to think of something to say.

"My testicles are sore" was all I came up with.

"Bloody prat" observed the Uncle, before moving on.

*

"Hey, hey," began again the testee on my right. "Hey. Who would you like to be assigned to?"

"Me?" asked the testee to my left. "I hadn't really thought about it."

"A cougar," said the testee on my right. "I want a nice, horny cougar."

The testee on my left giggled in delight, agreeing, "Yeah, a cougar. A cougar. Wait! How about a red-head? A red-head!"

"Blonde!" argued the testee on my right, getting himself into a frenzy. "Blonde!"

"No wait, wait!" Lefty interjected, seemingly having stumbled upon a revelation. "What about tits?"

"Nobody is going to be assigned to anyone," I explained, bringing to an end the nonsense.

"You what?" asked Righty.

"The chances of being fertile are so slim, that even if there were a thousand of us in here, which there aren't, the likelihood would be that only one of us would be fertile, and odds are it wouldn't be one of us three. Now, good night."

I turned over to get to sleep.

Righty burst into tears.

"You mean we'll be assigned to sweep nuclear waste?" he whimpered.

This set Lefty off, who added, "And we'll be dead within a week!"

"Six months or more," I advised with a yawn.

"No, it's down to one week on average," cried Lefty. "On account of there being ever more waste to sweep. Some aren't lasting a day. They're coming down with boils. Their heads are melting."

I admit this was news to me. I sat upright in bed. Righty and Lefty were bawling, attracting the attention of the testees who lay in close proximity, who in turn started to whisper, weep and wet themselves. One week does seem rather more immediate than six months.

"Shut up!" shouted the Uncle, now at the far end of the hall.

"Calm down," I whispered to the group. Calling attention to ourselves wasn't going to help our cause. "It's all right."

I'd created this stir. I realised that it was up to me to return us to calm, despite the growing anxiety in the pit of my stomach, probably forming itself into an ulcer, at the suggestion that my head will have melted by the end of the week.

I ruffled through my rucksack and pulled out what I always use to calm myself in times of distress, loneliness and despair.

"It's a book," observed Righty.

"With words and that?" sniffled Lefty.

"Yes, with words and that," I confirmed.

It wasn't just any book. It was the book my mother used to read to me when I was a small boy. It was the book she left behind for me. It was my last memento of her - a piece of her that was still with me.

"I'll read a story. It'll take our minds off the other stuff," I said, hopefully.

The testees gathered round as I showed them the cover, "Jacqueline and the Beanstalk."

Opening the book to the inside cover, I cast a glance at the inscription from my mother, written in defiance over the stamp of approval from the Ministry of Communications, the words "Reach for the Sky."

*

"Once upon a time," I began "Jacqueline and her mother lived in poverty, because Jacqueline's dead-beat dad abandoned them. That was what men did in those days."

I turned the page, and continued to read.

"All they had in the world was a cow, called Body. Body the Cow. One day, an old man in the market exploited Jacqueline's poverty, by forcing her to sell her Body in exchange for some beans."

The testees were calmed. Some began to yawn.

"The beans grew into a tall, erect beanstalk, which Jacqueline immediately mounted. The beanstalk vibrated in the wind, but Jacqueline managed to climb it all the way to the top."

I turned the page.

"There she met a wealthy giant. Jacqueline robbed the giant of everything that he had, which quickly led to the giant plummeting to his death, all of which was ok, because he was a man. The end."

I looked around at my fellow testees. All had returned to their beds. Some were fast asleep. Others were dozing off with their eyes closed, smiles spread across their faces. Most were peacefully relaxed, and had resumed farting. Others were masturbating uncontrollably.

I never tired of that book, or of its inscription, "Reach for the Sky."

The day after my mother wrote the inscription, she left home to join the circus. She wanted to give the trapeze a try. I was left with my neighbours, a kind, elderly couple, who took me in, and gave me the chores their bodies could no longer manage - trips to the grocery store, cleaning the house, fixing the roof. They called me "The Milk Maid."

Word arrived from the circus, a week later, that my mother had died in a tragic accident. It turned out that she wasn't very good at the trapeze, and had forgotten to hold on.

The details, as far I received them, were that her body had bounced off an elephant and landed headfirst in a popcorn stand to the horror of a packed crowd. It was an image that will live with me for the rest of my life.

CHAPTER THREE

STUD RAMROD

I was the last testee to enter the results room, a converted classroom by the look of it, and this immediately drew disapproving glances my way from the two Uncles who stood at the front, one being Uncle Joe, who's unorthodox yet effective method of releasing my juices had left my testicles looking like two shriveled dates, and the other Uncle Jim, who had been patrolling my line the night before. The testess sat cross-legged on the floor.

The pain emanating from my gonadal area meant that I could now only move at a slow waddle, and so I had been left behind while the other testess had skipped ahead to get their results, still seemingly buoyed by delusion in regards to the inevitable outcome.

I'd struggled to keep up, and was panicked that my tardiness would call the attention of the Uncles, and the testees, my way. Luckily, when I arrived, the Uncles were delivering a mantra in full swing and seemingly didn't want to pause.

"Why does the human race face extinction?" asked the Uncles.

"Because of men," answered the testees, dutifully.

"Why are the earth's resources depleted?" they asked.

"Because of men," answered the testees.

"Why is the population infertile?"

"Because of men."

The Uncles looked my way.

"Why are you late?" they asked.

"Um, because of men?" I answered, thinking on my feet.

This triggered a roar of laughter amongst the testees and looks of scorn from the Uncles, as my face turned a dark crimson to match the shade of my testicles.

"Because he's a late-cummer, get it?" roared one of the testees. "That's why you had to squeeze his balls out!"

This really was classic banter.

*

"Over here, blueberries," said one of the testees. It was the giant who'd already filled his swill bucket when I arrived in the testing cubicle. He motioned to a space next to him on the floor. I waddled over, tried to sit down, and rolled onto my back like a helpless beetle.

This drew more laughter from the testees. The Uncles, who were less amused, screamed at me to stop it. "Stop what?" I wondered. Did they think I was doing this on purpose?

"Now," said Uncle Joe. "Uncle Jim will read out the results of your test. Those of you who are found to be fertile will be assigned to a Commandress, to fertilize her blessed eggs with your mighty seed. Those of you who are infertile will be sent to sweep nuclear waste all day, until you are dead."

Uncle Jim motioned to two doors at the side of the room. One had the notice "Studs" on the front, under the silhouette of an erect penis, the other had the notice "Duds," under a silhouette of a limp penis. I believe we had all got the point.

"Number One!" called Uncle Jim, reading from a sheet.

Number One, a lanky testee close to the back, hopped up and bounded to the front. He stood beside Uncle Jim, shifting from side to side, seemingly unable to contain his excitement.

"Alright?" asked Uncle Jim.

"Yup," answered Number One.

"Confident?" asked Uncle Jim.

"Quietly confident," said Number One.

Uncle Jim read from the sheet, and announced to the crowd, "Dud Limplick."

"Nooooo!" screamed Number One, the newly named Dud Limplick, quite unbecomingly. "Whyyyyyyyy?"

Uncle Joe shoved a broom into Limplick's hands and pushed him towards the door with the limp penis.

It was going to be one of those days.

*

The previous night, when I finally had gotten to sleep, my dreams were haunted by images of melting faces, the thought of inhaling toxic fumes and the growing immediacy of certain death. I awoke in a sweat.

Sweeping nuclear waste, the nearer it approached on my horizon, was losing its appeal. I had to remind myself of the horrors of the alternative - a life "out there" spent serving "them." I assured myself, over a buffet breakfast, that one's face melting probably sounded worse than it was. Besides, sweeping nuclear waste all day would give one time to think - to ruminate on the deeper mysteries of life and the Universe.

Meanwhile, my fellow testees complained about the breakfast. Eggs floated in a tray of oil, the bacon was overcooked. One witty testee commented that the complex was a converted agricultural school - the cattle barn, the sports hall, the classrooms - ironic then, that they were serving food that wasn't fit for animals.

Those at my table became particularly aggressive when the buffet ran out of toast. I had to calm them by assuring all that I would write an angry letter addressed to whomever was in charge, pointing out the failings of the breakfast, with some mention of other passing indignities inflicted at the centre, and that I would expect them to bring about real change. Satisfied with this, the testees drank their coffee without any further grunts.

It's important to think positive. It aids digestion.

"Number Forty-Seven!" called Uncle Jim, losing no enthusiasm as the morning dragged on. So far, forty six testees, forty six Duds. Totally unsurprising. Forty-Seven was the giant next to me - the only one of us, if physique was anything to go by, who had a chance of being a Stud. I was Forty-Eight.

Forty-Seven bounded to the front.

"Excuse me, ladies," he laughed as he saluted us farewell.

Both Uncle Joe and Uncle Jim looked up to Forty-Seven with a mix of awe, wonder and hope. And then Uncle Jim read from his sheet.

"Dud Wimpole."

The disbelief, despair and shock which filled the room didn't just come from the two Uncles. It came from all of us. I think we had all, by then, hoped that this ordeal would have produced at least one Stud. I mean, otherwise what was the point?

"What?" roared Wimpole. "I 'aint no goddam Dud!"

"Take the broom," said Uncle Joe, resigned.

"I impregnated a horse," bellowed the furious Dud, taking the broom and snapping it between his fingers. "A male horse!"

The Uncles hung their heads in despair as the mighty, yet deemed-to-be-infertile behemoth, took to the door, the one marked "Duds."

"Right, who's next?" asked Uncle Jim, totally broken now, and almost forgetting to consult the sheet. "Oh well, then, Forty-Eight."

In a process that took no more than four minutes, I struggled to my feet, adjusted my glasses, pulled my gown tightly over my squashed testicles, and waddled to the front, while the Uncles and the remaining testees looked at me with utter despair, as though all the disappointment in the human race rested on my frail shoulders.

Imagine all of our surprise then, when Uncle Jim read out:

"Stud Ramrod!"

CHAPTER FOUR

DUD WIMPOLE

Once someone gets an idea into their heads, it's very difficult for them to change their minds, no matter how obviously wrong the initial idea, and no matter how obvious the truth.

When Uncle Jim read out from his sheet that I, Forty-Eight, was the potent impregnation machine, "Stud Ramrod," the idea seemed to be planted irreversibly into his and Uncle Joe's brains, buried deep, the shovel thrown away.

And no amount of calm and rational pleading from myself that I was clearly not a Stud, and that the results were faulty, most likely mixed up with Forty-Seven's, and that he was probably Stud Ramrod, and that I was therefore Dud Wimpole, was able to dispel the myth that had seemingly taken over their psyches.

"So modest," stated Uncle Jim.

"The finest Studs are," Uncle Joe added, before shoving me towards the door marked Studs.

The door itself was too heavy for me to push open, fortified, as it was, out of iron, and obviously designed for much stronger men.

"Just give it a shove," called Uncle Jim.

I pressed my whole body against the thing and managed to squeeze through a tiny crack, almost knocking my glasses off in the process.

"Magnificent," I heard Uncle Joe say to the still shocked and disbelieving group of testees before him.

Panic set in on my part when it became clear that the Uncles really weren't getting it, that they actually were entertaining the notion that I was a Stud, and that I was really being directed down the path of a fertilizer of Commandresses.

I remember the exact moment when the penny dropped for me. I was sent to a training dojo, where I and a dozen designated Studs were given false moustaches, a bottle of cologne and a programme of indoctrination and instruction on both how to please and impregnate a Commandress.

It didn't go well.

*

"You are the chosen ones!" Uncle Joe announced to us, a bunch of prats, standing obediently before him. "The saviours, the rescue squad. The future of mankind rests in your able testicles."

I sneezed. The fake moustache was itching my nose.

"The most important thing to remember from the Future Fertiliser Induction Programme," continued Uncle Joe. "Is that you are expected to remain attractive at all times, to project an air of allure at every moment, to be ready to fit into your Commandress's busy schedule and to be ready to spunk up in seconds."

He was such an odd man.

"You," Uncle Joe singled me out. "Are you projecting an air of potency, allure and irresistibility?"

"No," I answered.

"Why not?"

"Because my nose is itchy, and I may have a cold." I answered. "And as I keep pointing out, I can't project potency. I can't even project sperm. I'm not a Stud."

"That's why you're here," announced Uncle Jim, rousing and insane. "To become Studs!"

"Utterly mental" I observed.

We then entered what they referred to as the Future Fertilizer Induction Programme, each element of which I failed, unsurprisingly and spectacularly.

Lesson One: Dancing. Uncle Joe instructed us to move our bodies in a way that was both "alluring" and "cool." This involved gyrating our hips in a ludicrous and unnatural fashion while trying to maintain a smirk at all times. Feedback on my performance was that I was making "dancing look like some sort of chore," which of course it was.

Lesson Two: Head Wobbling. Apparently these experts had determined that wobbling one's head from side to side while talking projects an air of suave sophistication. I told them that it made us look like the tendons in our necks had been severed. The Uncles reminded me that failure to please our Commandresses would result in us actually having the tendons in our necks severed.

Lesson Three: Moustache Maintenance. Self-explanatory. Pointless.

Uncle Jim went through our fitness routine - Studs were expected to perform 1,000 sit ups and 1,000 press ups per day, or as many as it took to induce a mild heart attack. We were told to follow a "body maintenance" plan loaded with terms which were foreign to me then, and remain foreign to me now: "side crunches," "supplement intake," "ab implants." I figured the less I understood, the better.

And then it was on to the highlight of the day, Uncle Jim explaining in extraordinary reverence the mating ceremony.

"You will be summoned to the bedroom of your Commandress," Uncle Jim began in hushed tones, while Uncle Joe dimmed the lights of the dojo and lit a candle, seemingly to set the scene. "There you will find the Commandress's husband, lying flat on the bed, facing upwards. You shall lay on the husband, your back on his front. When she is ready, your Commandress will enter the bedroom, and mount you. Your seed will flow into her blessed juices, and fertilize her holy eggs with your life force. A child will be conceived. Humanity will be saved."

"Bloody ridiculous," I pointed out.

"Now, who wants to get tattooed?" asked Uncle Jim, turning the lights back on.

The trainee Studs cheered, confirming their idiocy, and Uncle Joe announced:

"Nothing raises female libido so strongly as jealousy, and nothing invokes jealousy quite like the name of a former lover tattooed on one's penis."

This got another cheer.

"I'm off, then," I said, and made for the door.

The next thing I knew, the Studs were pinning me down on the mat, and the two mad Uncles were hovering over my nether region with a tattoo gun.

"What was her name, then?" asked Uncle Jim.

"Vivi," offered the Studs. "Talula, Lilly-Mae…"

Uncle Jim leaned in.

*

"You passed out, again," said Uncle Joe.

"Yep," I confirmed, standing before him in his office.

"Second time in three days," the mad Uncle ruminated. "Almost like the heroine in a Victorian novel, prone to passing out with a touch of the vapours. Not very Stud like behaviour, is it?"

"Nope," I agreed. "That's because I'm not a Stud."

Uncle Joe nodded at me, thoughtfully.

"We only managed three letters."

I looked down through my red garment to inspect the work. He was right.

"Lil," it read, permanently etched into my penis.

"Lil," said Uncle Joe. "You know, your complete failure to perform any of the tasks presented to you is remarkable. It's a level of defiance the likes of which we've never seen."

"It's not defiance," I explained. "It's incompetence."

"Remarkable. Absolutely remarkable," said Uncle Joe rising from his chair, and coming round the front of the table to stand opposite me.

"Do you believe in destiny, Stud Ramrod, or Dud Wimpole, or whoever the hell you are? Do you believe in fate? You see, when you know as much about the past as I do, you start to see patterns. You start to see inevitability. Let me give you a little lesson in…" and Uncle Joe whispered this banned word. "History."

I let out an involuntary yawn.

It's not that I wasn't curious about the past. It's just that obtaining an accurate and fair account of anything that had happened pre-present times had become so difficult, any attempts to do so seemed to result in mere ridiculous speculation. At the time of my youth, items from the past still lingered in the culture, wonderful stories about an imagined future, with space travel and justice, inspiring stories about long ago, but eventually these were phased out, along with any word with "His" in it. The only mention at school of the past came in reference to former talent show competition winners, the names of whom appeared on every standard test.

"I'll ignore the yawn," said Uncle Joe. "That's the conditioning."

He had a point. Maybe I would learn something from this.

CHAPTER FIVE

AN UTTERLY POINTLESS HISTORY LESSON

"The century before the nuclear war, the 20th, was characterised by the battle of the sexes," began Uncle Joe. He flicked a switch on a projector, and illicit images in black and white flooded the far wall. They depicted a woman repeatedly slapping her husband across the face, accompanied by an off screen mechanical laugh.

"The few historical records which survived the war show us, by the early 1900s, women had gained equal rights in the home..."

Images flooded the wall featuring written laws on right of property, right of income, Saint Mary Wollstonecraft, men being slapped.

"Finding these newly empowered women impossible to live with, men engaged in a World War, just so they could get away. They called this The Great War, which shows how much they must have loved it."

Uncle Joe switched to grainy footage: troops of soldiers in England, France, Germany, all looking very happy.

"These men returned to women who were now emboldened, having held the responsibility of the household while the men were away, and having held affairs with the soldiers of occupying armies."

Archive footage now showed women on protest marches, men in sitcoms being slapped, and satisfied looking war-time wives.

"And so men quickly started up a second World War!"

The footage now showed happy and proud looking soldiers of all races, embracing, shooting guns, flying spitfires and waving flags.

"Men flocked from around the world to take part in this war, such was the global spread of female empowerment."

An animated map illustrated the movement of World War 2 forces.

"By the middle of the century, women had established the right to vote in countries across the globe. This was the beginning of the end for democracy, and the rise of elected leaders around the world with moustaches."

The images of moustached leaders flooded the wall, along with their titles: Adolf Hitler of Germany, Margaret Thatcher of England, Tom Selleck of Hawaii...

"Women gained rights in the workplace, and they soon held posts in government, in law, and even as airline pilots, as this footage probably shows."

Uncle Joe showed footage of planes flying into two twin towers in New York.

"Men responded in protest by dressing like cartoon characters and climbing up buildings."

The archive footage showed men dressed in red spider costumes, scaling buildings, carrying flags that read "Fathers For Justice."

"When this surprisingly did not work, men responded in the only way they knew how. They blew everything up."

The archive footage displayed missiles and nuclear bombs signifying the War.

"Women and children hid in underground tunnels."

Photos flickered across the wall of women and children entering the tunnel. Some women were pregnant.

"They stayed down there for three years. Time passed. Children were born."

One particularly striking photo depicted a mother placing a pair of horn-rimmed glasses on her child.

"Women and children emerged from the tunnels. Of the surviving race, women outnumbered men 100 to 1.

A photo depicted a few men cowering under a tent.

"A new world was born. A new world order. A world order run by women."

The images displayed proud and determined looking women.

"Boys, like yourself, were sent to underground school and were taught only of their evil. They became men and were sent to office blocks to serve women."

An image of an office block covered the wall with an interior sign reading "Floor 83. Officers charged with texting women all day."

"Society flourished, until it was discovered that the nuclear war had left the human race on the brink of infertility."

A petri dish filled the wall: A single sperm quivering alone, wearing glasses.

"The women consulted the Head Brain for advice. Men were separated into two categories, those who were still fertile, the Studs, and those who were not, the Duds. And then things really went to shit."

CHAPTER SIX

WHAT'S IN A NAME?

"Why are you telling me this?" I asked the silly chap, having nodded my head in politely feigned agreement to his pseudo-history lesson.

"Can't you see? Can't you see?" asked Uncle Joe, twice. "When you take a step back from history and look at it from a distance, the gas bubbling, the inevitability pushing through. You could be the cork at the top of that champagne bubble. You could be Stud Ramrod."

The pressure of sporting a moustache all day had clearly driven the man insane, I determined, and the earlier I was away from his presence the better.

"Maybe those results were mixed up for a reason, if indeed they were," the lunatic continued. "Maybe you were destined to go out into that world, venture forth into the heart of Dileag, that world totally controlled and dominated by women, with men cowering... Yes?"

I had my hand up to ask a question.

"Can I have a quick bathroom break? My bladder is unreliable."

"Look, maybe you are Dud Wimpole. Or maybe you're Stud Ramrod. Either way, we're faced with a choice here. You can be retested. And if you're found to be a Dud, so be it, a certain and immediate death awaits you on the nuclear waste dump. Or you choose to accept the mantle. Be Stud Ramrod. You go out there into

Dileag, and you at least have a chance of a not so immediate death."

"I don't understand why you'd allow that to happen?" I told him, peeing a little.

"Your non-subservience, your insubordination - it gives me hope, Dud Wimpole. I haven't had hope for a very long time."

*

I remember the moment I made my choice. The inner workings of the mind behind any of our decisions are never easy to unpick. I really feel that trying to explain one's exact motives or actions is about as futile as a history lesson from Uncle Joe. However, the precise moment I decided - that I can tell you.

The fellow Stud trainees and I were back in the classroom, covering a module on restaurant etiquette. We were to learn the ins and outs of how to wine and dine a lady and how to maximise her evening entertainment while minimising our chances of having gravy thrown at our faces.

The room was furnished with temporary circular tables, arranged in close proximity, with two Studs at each table and facing each other. This allowed, while the Uncles filled jugs with gravy at the front of the class in preparation for role-play, for conversation to arise.

I listened to Studs reminisce with each other about a life they were leaving behind. It was a life of prescribed regularity and total uniformity, and yet, it was spoken of in tones of wistful nostalgia. Their voices merged into one.

"I had a nice job, making cupcakes all day. And then at the end of the shift, my lady boss would come along to my cubicle and stamp on them all."

"I had a nice apartment. 1 metre by 1 metre. It had a stain on the carpet. I miss that stain."

"I used to ride to work on the bus. A red one. I like red ones."

It was the same life. All of us had the same life. I said as much under my breath, to myself.

"You what?" asked the Stud opposite me.

"Nothing," I said.

Their existence was horrible. It was for us all. It couldn't go on like this. A change was necessary, and somebody would have to bring about that change. That person obviously wouldn't be me, and I had absolutely no interest in it being me.

That said, having one's face melted off is something that one should avoid for as long as possible, a point which was hammered home a few moments later when the trainee Stud opposite me threw a jug of hot gravy in my face for not giving him enough attention, and that was before we even started the role-play.

*

Uncle Joe and Uncle Jim stood in front of me with hugely benign looks of pride on their massive and insane faces.

"Put this on," said Uncle Jim, sliding a red gown, with a ludicrously oversized hood, over my head.

"You look marvelous," said Uncle Joe, almost tearing up.

I looked like a cross between Little Red Riding Hood and the Grim Reaper.

"Don't forget this," said Uncle Jim slapping a newly washed fake moustache onto my face.

I looked like a cross between Little Red Riding Hood and the Grim Reaper, who just happened to be wearing a fake moustache.

The moustache smelled of laundry detergent, and this made me think of my former neighbour, who had worked in the Department of Fake Moustache Washing, and who always smelt of lavender, to which I am allergic.

I sneezed.

"Through this door, is Dileag," announced Uncle Joe. I had no idea what door he was talking about. We were standing in a small, square room with four white walls, which may have well been padded.

"The core of our female led society, the center of the city, The Big Vulva," he continued, surely making some of this up as he went along.

"You have been lucky enough to have been assigned to the household of one of Dileag's foremost and highest ranking officials, Commandress Roseanne," added Uncle Jim from his ever present clip-board. "Your mission, to please her, to account to her every need, and to impregnate her mighty ovum!"

"And if you can do that, you have a good chance of leading a life that may be better than nuclear toxic overwhelm," added Uncle Joe. "As long as you manage to do it by the end of the month?"

"What happens at the end of the month?"

"Her magic lady time," chorused the two nutcases in unison. "Her blooming rose magnificence, her colourful tirade upon her thighs."

"And if you fail to please her at that time - Women's Wrath!" shouted Uncle Joe. Uncle Jim flinched, as though experiencing convulsions, and I began to whistle.

"Why are you whistling?" asked Uncle Jim, quite understandably.

"I whistle when I'm nervous."

"Don't whistle, it drives them mad. They see it as a sign of happiness, of freedom. Women's Wrath!" screamed Uncle Joe again, sending Uncle Jim into a kind of upright fit.

"Well, listening to you two is making me more nervous," I observed. "Where's the door?"

Uncle Joe shoved a wicker basket into my hands and pushed against a wall.

"Good luck to you," he said, as the light of the outside flooded the room.

"For all our sakes."

PART TWO

CONFLICT

CHAPTER SEVEN

INTO DILEAG

As the two mad Uncles shoved me out the door, my eyes adjusted to the light, and to the captivating figure ahead of me. Leaning against a limousine, dressed in skin-hugging black, the figure tossed back her long blonde hair over lithe but strong shoulders.

She could only have been in her early twenties, judging by her dainty thighs, her small but supple breasts, her waist, not yet expanded to full capacity but displaying the elegance of curve only enjoyed by her gender, and yet she displayed the composure and deportment of someone with immense and formidable power.

"Commandress Roseanne," I said, holding out my hand.

"That's her limo driver," Uncle Joe corrected, "Nicolette."

Nicolette threw back her head and laughed to the sky, and this reminded me that despite the severe psychological pressure on the feminine brain that had come with the burden of unilateral power, and the grotesque results of this power on the women of the world and on the world itself, it still felt good to hear a woman laugh.

"What a twat," observed Nicolette, and I knew instantly that she meant me. Then she added, quite rightly, "Why's he staring at my ankles?"

My eyes, I must admit, did seem to have lingered upon Nicolette's form for quite an awkward amount of time. We must have been approaching five minutes, now.

I don't know if it was the fact that I realised I was on the cusp of a monumental event and felt the obligation to record every detail as best as my memory would allow, or that I had spent an unhealthy amount of time solely in the company of men, but even with the two Uncles now staring at me, I seemed unable to tear my eyes away from Nicolette's ankles as I racked my brains for a way in which they could best be described.

"Dud - I mean, Stud Ramrod," Uncle Joe prodded me with his finger.

"Golf balls," I said, as though in a trance.

Nicolette cracked up again and walloped me on the ass as I scrambled into the limo.

She was just obeying custom.

*

"I have ADD," announced Nicolette, as she steered the limo away from the curb to the sound of screeching tyres, having neglected to release the handbrake.

"The bra size?" I asked, quite innocently.

"Attention Deficit Disorder," explained Nicolette. "Keep talking or I'll fall asleep."

This was as terrifying as it was endearing, zooming, as we were, the wrong way up a one way street.

"Ah, ok, I began," adopting my most playful and excited tones. "Breakfast today was…"

"Boring!"

Nicolette spun the car around a corner, knocking over a fire hydrant, a tampon bin and a mirror-booth, and sending my glasses flying into the air in the process.

"Ok, ok. Here's something exciting. Did you know that scientists used to say, I mean before science was banned for being too logical, that interdimensional travel could be achievable…?"

"Oh my… boooring," groaned Nicolette, throwing her head back as though ready to take an urgent nap.

"Ah, so you know, apparently I'm here to save the world."

"You're so boring!" wailed Nicolette, landing the car safely after she'd driven us at top gear over a speed bump. "Quick, take a photo of me."

She turned and handed me a mobile phone, abandoning any hope of steering the car, or of us surviving the ride.

"Why?" I asked, which under the circumstances was perhaps not helpful.

"You're so dumb! Just take a hot photo of me!" Nicolette screamed, through a pout-lipped, wide-eyed expression which, if I'm to be honest, looked a little forced.

I took the photo. Nicolette snatched the phone from me to inspect the result, and to provide useful feedback as we entered a tunnel.

"You're rubbish at everything!" Nicolette screamed in disappointment, a bold supposition based on the failings of one photograph, but one, admittedly, to which I have little argument.

Nicolette allowed the car to bounce off both sides of the tunnel as she held her camera up above her head and took a photo of herself to enable a glimpse of her cleavage within the frame.

It occurs to me in writing the above paragraph that those of you reading this at a different time and in a different place may find the behaviour I have just described hard to understand, and even now I have no idea what the purpose of this self photographing was.

You'll just have to trust me that this behaviour was a cultural quirk of that time and place, and is just one of more strange and outlandish elements of my overall account. I hope this does not detract from the obvious veracity of the rest of my testimony.

Upon exiting the tunnel, and having amassed enough photographs of her cleavage to satisfy whatever motives she may have had, Nicolette brought the car to a sudden halt a few meters away from a busy four way junction, causing my head to career off the partition dividing the passenger seats and the driver.

"Seat-belts banned?" I observed.

"They wrinkle clothes, duh," explained Nicolette.

The traffic signals, a glaring rainbow of multicoloured lights, flashed from red, to pink, to blue, to lavender… A mechanical voice announced from the light-box:

"Go at the colour that best reflects your mood."

"Hmm, I think I feel quite purple," Nicolette ruminated as she stamped down the accelerator and shot across the four way junction, leaving a towering pile up of cars in our wake and confirming, if any confirmation was needed, that I'd have been safer to have gone with the face melting.

*

I regret that while being thrown around the back seat of the car, I had little chance to observe the features of inner Dileag, this being the first time I had been granted access to anything other than the non industrial outskirts of the city. This was where the important decisions got made, it's where the big wigs lived, and in regards to the few women I did see out in the open of inner Dileag, I do mean this literally, they were all wearing very big wigs.

From what I did see of Dileag, I could ascertain that whatever affluence the collective industry of our society created was concentrated into this central area.

Malls gave way to more malls, which gave way to mega malls. Each glittered in gold and silver more opulently than the next. Their architecture honoured the female form. Domes were particularly popular and seemed to sprout from every roof, topped off, in many occasions, by an erect nipple made of solid diamond.

Some of these "nipples" had huge metal rings carved into them, as though awaiting giant women to come along and pick the domes up by the "nipple rings" and walk away with malls as though with shopping bags.

Some malls featured cinemas, often built into the roof domes. All were showing "A Trip to the Shops, Part 83." Smaller, connecting streets between malls, alternated between coffee shops, boutiques and shoe shops. Some were home to a decorative fountain, modeled in the shape of a vagina, spraying coffee onto the passing public.

A stadium took pride of place in the centre of the city and was highly visible as we shot the wrong way up an elevated expressway. The electronic red ticker-tape display around the stadium announced upcoming events: "Morning Ritual," "Public Hanging," "Bake Sale."

The expressway took us to a domestic street, lined with mansions, and the limo screeched to a halt in the driveway of the most imposing and rich of these mansions, the home of Commandress Roseanne.

Nicolette announced our arrival by smashing through the gates of the mansion and crashing into the garage.

CHAPTER EIGHT

TO IMPREGNATE A COMMANDRESS

It's very difficult to maintain one's dignity when clambering across the floor of a limo in search of one's glasses, while also dressed in an oversized red tunic. Nicolette observed this humiliation while holding the door open, waiting for me to exit the car, and as soon I retained my glasses from the floor and placed them back on my nose, she gave me a customary wallop on the ass which sent the glasses flying off again.

"You don't act very much like a Stud," Nicolette observed.

"Well, that's no wonder," I concurred, finally making it out of the car with not a shred of dignity intact.

She'd made a good point, of course. How on Earth was I to maintain the facade that I was a Stud? My training had been a total disaster. Nicolette was already suspecting that I didn't quite fit the mold. What hope could I have when I actually had to face the Commandress? What were the punishments for impersonating a Stud? I feared I could be in line for quite a telling off.

There was no time to alleviate my panic with anything resembling a plan, for we now stood outside the mansion door, graced with an iron bell, down from which dangled an obscene iron penis and pair of testicles.

Nicolette swung the iron cock and balls and sounded the bell.

"Welcome home," she added.

The door was opened by a half-man, half ape creature dressed only in a pair of white underpants and a top hat. This was Marku, man-servant to Commandress Roseanne, and an oddity even in the mad world to which I had found myself in.

This hairy-backed creature seemed to have been kept by Commandress Roseanne part as a general servant, part as a one-man circus exhibit to entertain guests.

"Greetings," Marku said, in an ill-fitting, high pitched drone, as Nicolette and I entered the house of horrors.

"I have been asked to introduce our guest to It. Where is It?" asked Nicolette, and Marku, seemingly understanding this curiously formed question, provided an equally odd answer.

"Here comes It."

A frail, withered man of undeterminable age joined us in the hallway, mincing out from the adjacent living room while rustling an upside down newspaper in an ostentatious show of I know-not-what.

He wore a lime green tunic, and sported a dyed brown moustache under a pair of unblinking, strangely round eyes. Nicolette did the introductions.

"Stud Ramrod, this is It. It, this is Stud Ramrod."

"Stud Ramrod," It sneered. "If you're a Stud, then I'm a…"

"House-husband," Nicolette interjected. "House-husbands are creatures found to be too inept even for nuclear waste sweeping and who are kept around homes as part of the furniture. This one came free with the sofa."

"Honour to meet you," I said, trying to be as polite as I could while already wondering how soon I could get out of this obvious lunatic asylum.

"Marku will show you to your room," said It. "No doubt our mighty Stud will want to powder his nose and fragrant his penis ahead of tonight's fertilization ceremony. The Commandress's ovulations have been most plentiful and we look forward to an imminent and successful display of potent prowess."

*

I paced the assigned room and checked the clock which hung on a wall, over a single bed. 11pm. I was to be summoned to the Commandress's chambers at the stroke of midnight. Marku had dropped me and my bag off at the room on the upper floor, and advised that I begin to pray.

All this was happening too fast.

My window looked out from the upper floor of the mansion, over a courtyard, to Nicolette's quarters above the garage. Nicolette's silhouette appeared at her window before drawing the curtains closed. Above the garage, clouds formed and disappeared at an unearthly rate. I pushed against the window. It was locked from the outside.

The clock chimed 12. I'd barely had time to unpack and unfold my underpants!

A sonorous knock sounded on the door.

I scrambled through the memories of the training centre. What had I learned in the Stud training?

Nothing.

Marku pushed open the door to the room. He was holding a candle. With a single finger, he motioned for me to follow him.

I tiptoed down the hallway behind Marku, to the entrance to Commandress Roseanne's boudoir. With a slow gesture of the arm, Marku signaled that I was to go inside.

The room was bathed in candle light, flickering off deeply rouge walls, rugs and bed-sheets. A stench of toxic perfumes and powders hung in the air. There on the bed was It, spread-eagled in a nightgown. Marku gave me a shove towards the bed and motioned for me to lie down.

Too terrified to think, I followed the Stud training, placed my glasses on the night-stand and laid down on It, my back to his front, trying not to fall off.

"Bloody ridiculous," I had to observe.

"Shhh," warned Marku, before disappearing from the doorway.

Suddenly, an imposing piece of classical music sounded through the room. The sound of anvils striking, a chorus chanting, a crescendo building. Smoke entered from the hallway. And through the smoke, at the doorway, she appeared.

Filling the frame entirely with her massive size, Commandress Roseanne appeared, a 20 stone behemoth with a determined, purposeful, lustful expression fixed on her face - a monster in lingerie. The behemoth lurched towards the bed and picked up speed, breaking into a sprint. She bounded into the air and hung there, over the bed, over me, for what seemed like the longest moment of my life, the final moment of my life…I screamed out loud.

Commandress Roseanne crashed down onto my body, onto It, onto the bed. The upper part of my torso snapped forward, my arms flailing in the air, my eyes seeing stars.

I screamed again, and cried.

I cried for help.

And I do believe at one point I squealed.

There was no longer any doubt: I had not made a good first impression.

*

My screaming created an almighty commotion in the boudoir.

Marku, followed by Nicolette, ran into the room alerted by the sounds of unimaginable horror that had emanated instinctively from the depth of my lungs. It cowered in the corner. I stood at the foot of the bed, trying to pull myself together.

Commandress Roseanne stood in front of me, towering over me in size, in stature and in a rage.

"What the hell is going on?" she bellowed.

"I'm impotent."

"How could you be impotent? You're a Stud!"

"It's not you, it's me."

"Damn right it's you. I'm the sexiest dancer in Dileag. I'm gorgeous!"

"She's gorgeous," wailed It, from the corner.

"I couldn't see you without my glasses."

"Glasses?" Commandress Roseanne roared in disgust.

This apparently was the final straw.

The last thing I remember from that night, having just managed to get my glasses back on, was the massive, engulfing fist of Commandress Roseanne flying towards my face and smashing into my nose.

CHAPTER NINE

HOPELESS

I spent the next morning in a strange and almost inexplicable sense of calm. I say almost inexplicable, because I am going to try to explain it now.

I believe this sense of calm was similar to that of a man being led to the gallows. The time for protest was over. The chance for hope was long gone. There was only the man, and a few short steps, between his neck and the rope which would end it all.

Such was my situation. I had made a blunder in entertaining the hope that I could impersonate a Stud for longer than five minutes. I had been, or would be, found out. The punishment, whatever that would be, was imminent. Failure was so inevitable, there was nothing else to do but to accept it, and to enjoy a final breakfast.

What surprised me was that the rest of the household seemed also to be in this resigned state. Rather than being greeted by the swinging fists of Commandress Roseanne when I entered the breakfast room, I found both It and Marku already at the table, heads down, looking forlorn.

"I used to be somebody. You know that?" It was saying. "I used to have my own desk. I had a 4x4 apartment. And now look at me. Part of the furniture."

"He has condemned us all," Marku added.

"Is there toast?" I asked.

"You are to go shopping," announced It, standing up, as though

49

repulsed by my presence, which I felt was a little harsh.

"I didn't know there would be shopping," I admitted.

"There will be shopping. Oh, there will be shopping!" And with that, It stomped out of the room.

"A Commandress can only reach the higher stratums of stati by having a child," Marku started to explain, as I began to wonder if breakfast was to be self-service or if there'd be a table option. "Recurring failings of a Commandress and her Studs will damage the reputation of a Commandress, and here, reputation is Queen."

While Marku was offering this profundity, he had been joined at the side by Niko, a lanky, cross-eyed fellow in an apron.

"Niko is a former Stud of Commandress Roseanne. Following his failures to produce a child, she kept him on to save face, citing his exceptional culinary skills," said the uncharacteristically talkative Marku.

Niko lay a plate of raw horse liver in front of me.

"I expect our new Stud will be hungry after a night of such virile demonstrations," suggested Marku.

"I'll see what I can scrape off the walls," said Niko, speaking, as it turned out, literally.

There I was, in the company of these idiots, when I could have been enjoying my last moments, perched atop a nuclear waste site, unbothered by anyone. What is life without a moment to ponder, to think? I could have been there, broom in hand, allowing my mind to wander to the far reaches of the Universe, with all of its infinite mystery.

Interspersed with this, I could have engaged my mind in another favourite pass-time, narrating my life story as though to an unseen audience, seated in rows somewhere in my head, perhaps eating popcorn, and only drifting from my narrative to occasionally check their phones.

"Why's he staring at the wall, like that?" Niko may have asked at this moment.

My hopeless fate had become the same hopeless fate of this strange and macabre household, with its perverse intimacies, its hostile frustrations and its grotesque eating habits. My failings would be their failings, their failings would be mine; we would share the same doom. In short, we were a family.

*

The resigned calm I'd felt at sunrise was shattered by late morning.

It didn't happen when I left the house, wicker basket in hand, passing Nicolette as she tried to mend the limo using duct tape. It didn't happen when I met Stud Longun at the street corner, the Stud who I was to go shopping with. He was a nice chap, a floppy haired fellow in his 20s, who thankfully guided me through the proscribed dialogue.

"God has brought us fine weather, this morning," he began, answering himself with, "for which we thank Her," as I looked blankly at the overcast skies.

It didn't happen when we entered the shopping district, the sidewalks into which were lined with beauty parlours and shoe shops, alternating with each other and stretching on into infinity. A crew of ladies dressed in overalls, perched on some scaffolding above one of the shops, called down to us amid wolf-whistles.

"Oi, show us a leg!"

Stud Longun gave an obligatory and coquettish giggle in return. He was good at this.

The ladies were fixing a poster on a billboard depicting a fully naked man, staring directly into the camera, with the caption reading: "Here is a naked man. Buy shoes."

Beside this, a second billboard displayed two naked men, staring directly into the camera. The caption read: "Two naked men. Buy make-up."

A third billboard simply depicted a naked man on a spit roast. The caption read: "Brought to you by the Ministry of Culture."

It didn't even happen when we passed the district park, a well manicured green space at the centre of the shopping district, that just happened to feature an array of what appeared to be bodies - men - 50 foot in the air, on spikes, with the spikes disappearing under their red tunics.

"Former Studs who failed their Commandresses," Stud Longun explained, noticing me turn pale. "Spike through the anus," and then collecting himself, "for which they deserved."

No, I finally snapped when I reached the grocery store, and it was another Stud who broke first.

Stud Longun and I joined a fairly long line which stretched out of the store and into the street. We waited, casually enough, observing the busy street scene. Shaven headed female guards patrolled the sidewalk, each carrying a long spike.

Down through the centre of the road, a Stud trotted along wearing a strange pointy hat, and dragging behind him, a proud looking Commandress, sat on a mobile throne on two wheels, attached to two sticks which the Stud carried in either arm.

"A successful Stud," Stud Longun whispered. "Those who successfully impregnate their Commandress get to parade their work around town, and wear a pointy hat."

"Well worth it."

At that moment, a middle aged Stud, exiting the grocery store with a plastic shopping bag in either hand, his wicker basket tucked under his arm, already full with shoes, broke. And this broke me. Or, more accurately, it was his shopping bags that broke. These flimsy plastic contraptions were seemingly designed to disintegrate on impact with anything heavier than a tissue, and the bags spilled the spoils of the grocery shop on the floor: broken eggs, smashed jars, fruit rolling off in all directions.

This appeared to be not the first time this had happened to that particular Stud, for as soon as the goods hit the floor, his back stiffened, his jaw tightened, he turned, and he stormed back into the store.

"It's environmentalism gone crazy," the Stud could be heard screaming from inside. "The flimsy, inane… they keep breaking."

A couple of guards ran into the store, spikes at the ready.

"How many times?" the Stud could be heard continuing. "Just give me a proper shopping bag! How difficult could it be? Just…" he could be heard saying, and then so could the sound of a sharp instrument, penetrating an orifice, and tissue, in a kind of squelching effect.

"Yep," said Stud Longun. "The ol' spike up the anus."

*

Before I knew it, my legs had carried me halfway across central Dileag and out of the shopping district.

"Where are you going?" Stud Longun pleaded, hurrying after me, trying to keep up. "We'll be caught!"

The truth was, I didn't know where I was going. Whatever had triggered the unfortunate Stud with the shopping bag had set me off. His breaking had broken me, and my legs were scurrying away before my mind, and Study Longun, could catch up.

"Where are you going?" Stud Longun continued to plead.

"I don't know," my legs may have answered as they carried me as far as the city wall - a solid, 100 foot monolith with barbed wire across the top.

"It's solid," I observed.

"It's a wall," Stud Longun explained.

Before I knew what was happening, my legs were carrying me back in the opposite direction, shooting across the city, back through the shopping district, past the stadium, and slap bang into the wall again.

"It goes all around," Stud Longun added, brilliant again.

I held my knees, part in exhaustion, part so they wouldn't fly off again.

"Now what?" asked Stud Longun, as I gasped for breath. "That was awesome. The adrenaline."

"What's left?" I managed to ask, through panting breath.

"Wall," Stud Longun, confirmed.

"Right?"

"Wall."

The truth is, when I've skipped lunch, my blood sugar wreaks havoc on my system and I can't function at all. Plus, if we were out too late, who knows how our respective Commandresses would react.

"Same again, tomorrow?" I suggested.

"Awesome," said Stud Longun, and we called it a day.

CHAPTER TEN

HOPE

Imagine my surprise when I found Uncle Joe waiting for me in my room when I returned to the mansion, the man who had convinced me to enter this bizarre women-led nuthouse of a city in the guise of a Stud, and the closest I had to a male mentor.

In fact, you won't have to imagine it, because I'll describe it now.

"Uncle Joe," I exclaimed, very, very surprised.

I added "How are you?" part with habitual politeness, part with the caustic irony of a man who had spent the afternoon avoiding penetrating anal spikes while shopping for eggs.

"Oh, not too good," Uncle Joe began. "It's Uncle Jim. He's grown out his moustache so his is longer than mine, now. I know why he's doing it. He's already winning the favour of Commandresses over me. In the coming months, I think he will try for a beard. It's…"

"What were you thinking?" I interjected, in the most measured and thoughtful tones I could muster given the circumstances. "I'm going to end up on a stick and displayed in the public park. I can't impersonate a Stud. Did you hear what happened last night? I'm going to be found out, I'm going to be killed. The squelching sounds. Squelch, squelch, squelch…"

"Calm down. I heard about your failings last night. That's why I'm here. I'm here to help." Uncle Joe fumbled around in his purse and brought out a pill. "This is for your penis."

"Pills make my eyes water."

"I've seen your Commandress; don't tell me you had your eyes open… Look, take this and you'll be able to get straight back into the mating ceremony."

"I don't want to get straight back into the mating ceremony. I want to get the hell out of here."

"There's an underground railroad," announced Uncle Joe. This was more like it.

"Where is it?" I asked.

"It's underground," said Uncle Joe.

Trying non-verbal communication, I jumped up and down and pulled out my hair.

"The station's right behind the stadium. The train goes underground, avoiding the walls. Successful Studs can travel to and fro to their next assignment, segregated from women passengers of course. There's a nice buffet cart…"

"Why didn't you tell me this before?" I asked, waving tufts of hair.

"I have a feeling about you, Stud Ramrod,"

"That's not my name!"

"I have a feeling you'll die a martyr."

"But I want to die a pensioner!"

"And besides, you're not going anywhere, tonight. The Commandress is still ovulating. The next ceremony is at midnight and you'll be expected to perform. You need that pill."

*

"Do me you little slut!"

Commandress Roseanne undulated her mountainous body on top of me, sending ripples through the mounds of her flesh, while roaring words of encouragement. "Do me or I'll have you killed!"

"I can't breathe," I wailed.

"No talking," advised It, the prickles of his moustache scratching against my neck. He was in tears, seemingly moved by the whole experience, and at the same time, being crushed to death, as was I.

The pill had taken control of my penis, which now had a life of its own, separate from my body, and defiantly immune to reality.

Uncle Joe had shoved me into the ensuite attached to my room so that our exchange would avoid detection. Studs were expected to be aroused simply enough by the delectable presence of their beauteous

Commandresses.

I'd taken the pill, a seemingly massive dosage, and my body had become instantly aroused as though in lustful appreciation of my toothbrush.

"You're a dirty piece of meat. Tell me you're a dirty piece of meat," roared the delightful lady. Was this a trick?

"No talking," I pointed out.

"You can tell her you're a dirty piece of meat," advised It.

"In that case, I am a dirty piece of meat," I stated.

"Waah haah haah," roared Commandress Roseanne, suitably delighted by the statement.

"I'm going to eat your face. I'm going to eat your face," she added cryptically, and then she bit me on the nose.

"The Earth's moving," cried It.

The Earth wasn't moving. An alarm was going off, and it was vibrating the whole mansion, right down to the bed-frame. The whole household came charging into the room, barely giving Commandress Roseanne time to cover herself and pound out of the room.

"The alarm," announced Marku. "Secure the mansion."

*

I scrambled back to my room, pulling my red tunic over a penis that still hadn't gotten over its appreciation of my toothbrush.

No sooner had I closed the door than I spotted the head of Stud Longun - perched atop a ladder outside my window. Longun pulled open the window from the outside.

"What the hell are you doing, here?" I wailed, as quietly as possible.

"I told my neighbour about our escape attempt. That was the greatest thrill of my life. I want to show you to him."

"I can only see your bollocks, Stud Longun."

This, it turned out, was the neighbour - Stud Mastall, a burly fellow perched further down the ladder, and well positioned to share in our imminent and collective execution.

"Stud Ramrod led us to the city wall, today. He'll lead us all out of the city!"

Stud Longun had clearly snapped. The alarm was ringing through the grounds of the mansion and all around us the sound of doors and windows being slammed shut echoed through the grounds.

"You're going to get us killed!" I pointed out, at risk of spoiling the surprise.

I had to think fast.

Was I to let them into the mansion and hide them in the room, risking exposure? Was I to give them direction and point them in the opposite direction, risking they be found in the grounds in the mansion? Or was I to lead them out of the mansion and grounds itself ensuring their safe exit?

As usual in the heat of the moment, I chose the worst possible option and climbed out onto the ladder.

We hid the ladder in some bushes and sprinted across the mansion grounds and out the main gate as quietly as could be, my penis pointing the way as though leading us into the night.

CHAPTER ELEVEN

GOOD SPORTS

By the time I was sent to school as a child, sports were on the way out.

In the interests of enforced equality, the concept of "winning" at races, games or physical activities had been outlawed, and as someone who struggled in each of these areas, that suited me just fine.

Medals were given simply for participation; to simply turn up was enough.

This was still not a satisfactory arrangement, however, as following the abolishment of segregation of sport participation - which could no longer be justified on the basis of an unmentionable physical superiority of one gender over another - it was observed that most of these sports resulted in one gender in particular winning, or participating better, than the other gender.

It was then so ordered that the consistently winning gender, myself excluded, would need to on purposely participate worse. The result was school running days in which boys would be required to slow themselves to a walk, allowing overfed young girls to plod ahead of them in running races, and other such non-events.

Enthusiasm for sports and games naturally waned under such arrangements and then sport was killed off entirely with the publication of the Charter of Anti-Masculinity.

The Head Brain took it upon herself to list attributes which were felt to be masculine by nature, including such items as "competitiveness," "aggression" and "being fast at running," and it was then observed that sports seemed to encourage all of these attributes, and so that was the end of sports.

The new generation was one that had not even been introduced to "the s word".

This was why it made perfect sense, I thought at the time, for myself, Stud Longun and Stud Mastall, to head straight to the old sports stadium, looking, as we were, for a place to converse without detection from city guards, and having snuck out of the mansion at night.

The stadium was now only used for morning ceremonies, hangings and bake sales, and luckily none of these took place after dark.

The two Studs and I found a way into the stadium via a turnstile and then emerged, through a corridor, onto the unused former football pitch. Under the moonlight, the pitch was far too illuminated and exposed for my liking, and so I scanned the place for the players' tunnel.

"Look-out, a bomb!" screamed Stud Mastall.

"No, this is a football," I explained to the young man, picking up the offending item. "You know, for play."

"Play? What is play?" asked the innocent fellow.

"Look, play," I said, throwing the ball to Stud Longun who instinctively caught it with two hands.

Longun then threw the ball to Stud Mastall who in turn caught it, and then tossed his head back in joy and laughed to the sky.

It was as though something had awoken in the two of them. Requiring no further instruction, the Studs were throwing the ball back and forth to each other, catching it perfectly, throwing it back, and galloping across the field as they did so.

They resembled two gazelles, elegantly prancing across the savannah, casting great silhouettes against the moon beyond, except that these gazelles were laughing, they were laughing with pure happiness and pleasure.

As they ran back and forth, engaged in such play, I could imagine a full orchestra playing some uplifting anthem to accompany the amusement and magnificence of the moment.

The whole thing came to an end when Mastall threw the ball to me and I fumbled the catch, allowing the thing to bounce off my head.

When I retained my glasses from the floor, I managed to spot the players' tunnel at the far end of the pitch, and it was there that we headed.

*

"Grenades!" screamed Stud Mastall.

"No, those are pool balls," I explained.

The players' changing rooms featured a pool table, centre of the space, and an array of sporting equipment in storage: balls, bats, surfboards, even hang-gliders - seemingly the entire remnants of a lost culture packed into one room.

"What do we do now?" asked Stud Longun.

"We hide," I explained.

"Awesome! And then what?" asked Longun, sitting down on a players' bench and seemingly hanging on my every improvised word.

"We run away," I suggested.

"Yeah!" Stud Mastall bellowed, in a deep, slightly affected voice.

"Where do we run to?" Longun probed, really stretching me at that point in time.

"The train station, perhaps." This raised a roar of approval, so I continued. "We'll need disguises."

"We can dress as chickens," suggested the odd Stud Mastall.

"No, not chickens, Stud Mastall. We'll need to disguise ourselves as successful Studs, who can move freely between assignments. Successful Studs do not dress as chickens." It was important that I really spell it out to these two.

"Beards!" cried Stud Longun. "My Commandress Rita wears wigs. We can repurpose them as massive beards."

"Well done, Stud Longun," I exclaimed, already picturing the three of us hanging dead from anal spikes, wearing fake beards well into the afterlife.

"But what about the hats?" asked Stud Longun, with rising excitement. "Successful Studs wear those pointy hats."

"I can steal some traffic cones!" Stud Mastall exclaimed, really coming into his own.

And there we had it: the three of us up dead on spikes, wearing fake beards and traffic cones on our heads; a final image.

What sounded like a drink can being kicked in a far off space shook us from our military-grade strategising and had us heading to the exit.

"Tomorrow, shopping trip, we'll go to the train station," I whispered, as we army crawled down the players' tunnel, perhaps unnecessarily, and out of the stadium.

*

It was the dead of night when I made it back to the mansion. The alarm had been deactivated, the grounds secured, the household presumably returned to their bedrooms.

I made it through the mansion gates without causing so much as a creak. The lock was permanently broken, thanks to Nicolette's charming quirk of driving through the gates without ever stopping, and so I was able to open a crack slightly and squeeze through.

A full moon made it impossible to shroud myself in darkness, and so I wanted to linger as little as possible. I made it across the mansion grounds with as fast a dash as I could muster.

I retrieved the ladder Stud Longun had brought to my window from the bush in which we had hidden it, and prodded the thing back up against the wall.

I began the ascent back up to my window, and, unbeknownst to me, I was being watched the whole time, as I stumbled back through my window, by Marku, peering from the shadows of his room.

I could never have imagined what the ramifications would be of Marku spotting me on that fateful night…

(It turned out the ramifications were very insignificant.)

CHAPTER TWELVE

UNDERGROUND RAILROAD

It was late morning at the rail station, and all was going brilliantly to plan. Stud Longun had brought the fake beards. Stud Mastall had provided the traffic cone hats. And in a last minute flash of inspiration, I'd made sandwiches. I'd gone for cheese and pickle for all, plus an apple each, and juice. You can't trust train food.

I'd made it out of the mansion without attracting too much attention from the menfolk, avoiding Niko's breakfast of what-might-be-ravioli, ignoring It's comment that I was a "cocky little bastard," and not even letting it bother me that the gorilla backed Marku was sitting at the breakfast table stark bollock naked.

The rail station was a hive of activity. Lady commuters strode to and fro across the concourse, picking up coffees, and then sprinting back the other way to buy pastries. Intermittently, a woman would step into one of the glass booths, signed as "Breakdown Boxes," and scream inaudibly while pulling her hair out.

Amongst all this, shaven headed, heavily tattooed female guards patrolled the space. Nobody actually seemed to be going anywhere, and I perhaps should have picked up on this before we entered the concourse and sought out the platform.

We immediately found ourselves swamped and surrounded by lady commuters, all eyes pointing our way, as may inevitably be the case when one is wearing a traffic cone upon one's head.

"We should have stolen some guns and blasted our way through," offered the ever thoughtful Stud Mastall through gritted teeth.

All was not lost, however. On a far wall, a train schedule was visibly nested between adverts of watches - with the slogan "So your Stud can count down to Women's Wrath."

A list of twenty or so trains, positioned in numbered platforms, all showed the same status: "Driver powdering her nose." However, it was the train at platform twelve which gave us hope, when its status invitingly switched to "Nose powdered."

"There's our exit," I exclaimed, and I led the two Studs across the concourse, shopping baskets under arm, penis ever erect, and I dare say I even started to whistle.

"Halt!" ordered a leather clad giant presiding at the entrance to platform 12. The giant, a bald headed female guard, stepped forward, cattle prod in hand, and flanked by an equally massive sun-burnt fellow guard on the right, and on her left, completing the trio, a guard with a face tattoo.

"Successful Studs!" continued the big bald one. "You didn't think we'd let you go without a kiss, did you?"

"No, no we didn't," I intervened, noticing my two comrades had been struck dumb at the sight of these monstrosities.

"Which of us would you like to kiss, first?" challenged the one with the face tattoo.

"Not that one," said the idiot Mastall, pointing at Sun Baked, before Stud Longun shut him up with a timely elbow to the ribs.

"We find you all equally beautiful, and fragrant," said I, coming in with the save.

What followed bears no detailed description - least not when I have already invited thoughts of sandwiches, but in short, the guards stepped up to the three of us, Big Bald on me, Sun Baked on Longun, Face Tattoo on Mastall, swept us off our feet, and tongued us.

Longun even got a shot of a cattle prod on the ass as we skipped away coquettishly and onto the platform.

*

Things went less well from that point on, because although the driver had, indeed, finished powdering her nose, she hadn't finished eating her lunch. I and the two Studs sat in an otherwise empty carriage for a full half hour, wondering what was going on, eating sandwiches, before we noticed that a small crowd had formed on the platform around the driver's compartment. We disembarked the carriage, and joined the group.

"I has cravings," the lovely lady driver was saying. "I has to eat when I has cravings."

"Excuse me, miss, how long does it take to satisfy these cravings?" I asked.

'Until I'm full or until I shit me-self," the driver clarified, helpfully.

Stud Longun quietly reminded Mastall and I that if we were out too long, the Commandresses would grow suspicious, and that we'd be told off, and then executed.

"Excuse me, sweet lady," I continued. "Would it be possible for you to kindly drive the train while eating?"

This, I felt, would do the trick.

"I can't be rushed!" explained the lady driver, loudly. "I'm hyperglycemic. I get dizzy spells."

"Oh for…" Stud Mastall, sadly got involved, with the unhelpful: "She smells of ketchup."

A venerable lady conductor stepped in at this stage, but even her expertise couldn't save the day. The driver was already screaming the word "abuse" like a siren.

"Oh dear," sighed the conductor. "This will go on all night. This train's going nowhere. Can I lick your face?"

"He called me fat, he called me fat," cried the driver, choking on her own words, and, it seemed, the remains of a hot-dog that had become dislodged from one of her cheeks.

I looked longingly down the track at a tunnel, and the darkness beyond. I half wanted to make a run for it there and then, but, as ever, eyes were upon us, the conductor, the commuters, the driver. The three of us charging into a tunnel with our fake beards and traffic cone hats would be bound to arouse suspicion.

We spent the afternoon pleading with the driver to no avail, until the first signs of evening began to darken the sky and mark the outer reaches of Dileag as beyond hope.

"What do we do now?" Stud Longun may have asked. I couldn't hear him clearly as the conductor had her sand-paper tongue lodged firmly into my ear.

"We give up," I explained, long overdue, and we parted, there and then, to return to our respective and personal hells.

*

My own personal hell was heating up by the time I got back to the mansion, with a party being thrown in the living room by Commandress Roseanne for a group of fellow Commandresses.

I entered the mansion dejected, defeated, and yet unprepared for quite how bad the evening was about to become.

"Where have you been?" bellowed Commandress Roseanne, beckoning that I join them in the living room. The fellow Commandresses lounged around on sofas and armchairs, glaring up at me in lustful hate. They were surrounded by recently opened boxes of lingerie.

I'm not sure what they were up to. I have never sat around with fellow males, unboxing our underwear, so I'm afraid I have no reference.

"The shopping trip has been most fruitful and much money has been wasted," I muttered - the standard reply.

Commandress Roseanne eyed me for a moment, as though contemplating how to proceed in my torture.

"This is Stud Ramrod," she announced, kind enough to introduce me. "Stud Ramrod is the worst fuck I've ever had."

The fellow Commandresses nodded with looks of utter non-surprise.

"Nice to meet you all," I said, hoping that was that.

"Strip for the girls," Commandress Roseanne ordered, sending a chill through my body which froze me to the core. "You heard me, strip."

The fellow Commandresses seemed to be pleased by this, as some of them started a clap to a beat, while others hollered at me to dance.

I managed a slight wobble of the head but apparently this wasn't enough because within seconds one of the Commandresses had pulled off my red tunic, which was the cue for the rest of them to start screaming the curious word, "Woo."

Luckily for me, Commandress Roseanne chimed in with some helpful suggestions:

"Gyrate those hips, gyrate those hips!"

"Woo, woo, woo!"

"Tie them to his cock!" - one of the Commandresses had found some tassels. One of the Commandresses obliged.

"Spin! Spin! Spin!"

And so there I was, naked in front of the Commandresses, a tassel tied to the end of my penis, gyrating my hips in a circle, swinging my penis, trying to make the thing spin.

"Tell us we're your victims!" wailed the Commandresses.

"You're my victims, you're all my victims," I gasped.

"Woo! Woo! Woo!"

All in all, it had turned out to be a pretty disappointing day.

CHAPTER THIRTEEN

COMMANDRESS ROSEANNE

You have to start questioning your life choices when you can no longer distinguish nightmares from reality.

For me, that moment came when Marku appeared in my room in the middle of the night and advised me that Commandress Roseanne had requested my presence in her boudoir.

I followed Marku down the hallway in my pyjamas, wondering where this particular nightmare/episode would lead.

Marku shoved me into the boudoir and closed me in with the monster.

Commandress Roseanne, sat behind a mahogany desk, feigned surprise to see me.

"Oh, Stud Ramrod, won't you sit down?"

She gestured with a mighty palm that I should take a seat across from her, on the opposite side of the desk.

The boudoir was a cross between an office and an opium den, with the work-desk taking pride of place in the centre of the room, silk cushions scattered across the floor, dark red drapes covering the windows.

The Commandress sat there staring at me, slowly tapping her meaty fingers on the table, breathing very deliberately through her nose. If I wasn't now leaning towards this all being a dream, a result of one too many cheese and pickle sandwiches, I might have felt quite awkward.

Instead, I allowed my eyes to wander the room.

The walls were decorated with oil paintings, each depicting a figurehead of the past, legendary leaders whose existence may or may not have been mythological, and yet whose presence and power was still very much felt in our day: Joan of Arc, Simone De Beauvoir, Vanessa Hudgens.

"Are you admiring her breasts?"

The Commandress was, of course, referring to Hudgens.

Joan of Arc was depicted as wearing metal armour and De Beauvoir was definitely flat-chested.

Hudgens was painted in a bikini.

'No, I only admire your breasts."

Now, this statement could have gone either way, seemingly challenging the line between Stud and Commandress as it was, but I took the Commandress's non-reaction as a sign that I was on the right track, and emboldened, I continued: "I was just reading the quote up there. 'Women are taking over. I feel like it's something we've recently discovered, true woman empowerment. It's a great thing.' - Vanessa Hudgens."

Commandress Roseanne and I looked up at the bikini-clad philosopher and we shared a moment of reverence for the profundity of the wisdom on offer.

Then, making her intentions known, with no further delay, Commandress Roseanne reached into her desk drawer.

My eyes darted across the room for a place to take cover, and finding none, my mind working like a flash, I quickly resolved to sit very still and try to take the bullet in the head, minimising pain, as well as the sight of my own blood, both of which make me queasy.

Commandress Roseanne, however, pulled from her desk, not a gun, but an equally terrifying weapon: some women's magazines from the turn of the century.

Each item was preserved in individual wrapping, and boasted articles such as "How to control your man," "How to control your orgasms," and "How to control your car."

"Do you remember these little beauties?" asked the Commandress, pushing the long-banned magazines across the desk for my viewing. It was as though she was sharing a dirty secret. "Magnificent, aren't they?"

What was the Commandress up to? Was this a test? I had no

choice but to feign interest in whatever it was the Commandress was showing me.

She turned the pages of one of the magazines as though she was handling an ancient scroll.

"Did you know they were dating?" asked the Commandress of a weird plastic faced couple grinning into the camera in one of the magazine's centre spreads.

"No, I didn't," I said. "Fascinating, isn't it?"

"He cheated on her, apparently," said the Commandress, as she stared into the eyes of the long-dead plastic faces, looking for I know-not-what. "These magazines were one of the few outlets women had in The Age of Oppression."

By Age of Oppression, she meant pretty much the whole of human history, labelled also, by some modern-day scholars, as The Epoch of Victimisation, right up to the Rise of the Labia.

The Commandress seemed to collect herself, as she gathered the magazines, tucked them away in the drawer, and sat back in her chair to resume staring at me, unnervingly.

"How was your day?" I asked, really stepping over the line now, but expecting to wake up or to be shot any minute, anyway.

This surprisingly seemed to resonate with the Commandress. I doubt many people make casual conversation with someone of such stature. My instincts told me that the Commandress was acting from a deep-rooted need to just talk.

"I don't want to talk about it," she said. "We just had a request from the Amazon Women of the Amazon. They want to send a delegation to see if we can open up some trade channels. That's all."

"Wouldn't that be interesting?"

"It's not something we've done before."

"How does the economy work here? I don't see much productivity." It was a question that had been playing on my mind since I'd entered Dileag. How many people actually did any work here? The Commandress seemed to enjoy the deference and the opportunity to show off her superior knowledge.

"It's a commerce-based society. It's based on consumption. We buy things. Then we buy more things. It's flawless."

"But where do you get the money from?" I asked.

"From bank loans!" A familiar hint of irritation had crept into Commandress Roseanne's tone - familiar to me in all my interactions with the fairer sex, yet still I could not resist.

"But what if the bank managers stop giving you loans?"

"We'll execute them!" explained the Commandress, the matter settled.

We sat opposite each other, each lost in thought. At the mention of a trade delegation, an image had flashed into my mind - an image of Commandress Roseanne, of all the Commandresses, distracted from their monitoring of men, their focus turned to the visitors, an empty train station, an absence of guards, a way out.

"Still, it would be nice to have some new stuff, wouldn't it? More trade agreements mean more shopping."

Commandress Roseanne nodded at me thoughtfully, caught herself in the action, and ordered me to piss off out of her room.

CHAPTER FOURTEEN

THE ARRIVAL

The trade delegation arrived in the afternoon.

The car-park outside the sports stadium was converted into a landing dock, and the people of Dileag lined up to greet the ships from the Amazon as they hovered gracefully on the tarmac.

The ships themselves were massive wooden constructions with flight upgrades, which allowed them to float from city to city.

The rumours were true: rather than executing the majority of their menfolk, assigning them to office work or sending them off to sweep nuclear waste, the Amazons had set their unfairer sex to focus on "ugly" tasks such as engineering, and as a result enjoyed the benefits of a technologically rich society that combined natural products with scientific advancement.

A marching band from Dileag greeted their arrival by performing the chorus from "Starships," by the revered composer, Nicki Minaj.

The ships were too large to land in the car-park, and so smaller docking ships emerged from their hulls, carrying five or six ambassadors at a time, and landing gracefully in front of the delegation from Dileag.

Commandresses took pride of place, lined up at the front to welcome the visitors, and behind them stood each of their households in a sea of Stud-red and husband-green - an odd bunch, indeed, flanked by guards and citizens. As I hoped, all the eyes of Dileag were on this momentous occasion.

The first visitors from the delegation stepped out of the docking ship and the crowd exhaled a collective gasp of awe.

The Amazon women were physically perfect, each over six feet tall, perfectly proportioned, with long flowing hair, high cheekbones and strong jaws. Their bodies - clad in knee-high boots, metal skirts, and figure-hugging bodices - like their hover ships, defied gravity.

The Commandresses of Dileag, immediately put to shame, collectively tried to suck in their pot bellies.

They simultaneously cast accusative glances at Commandress Roseanne, who in turn looked over her shoulder at me, with a glare of absolute venom. I could fully count on a punch on the nose from the Commandress at her earliest opportunity.

Things only got worse when the Chief Delegate, Queen Iyana, stepped out of the landing ship.

Spear in hand, hair tossed over her strong, young shoulders, she cut a figure that exceeded even the magnificence of her fellow people.

Yep, she'd create a distraction all right.

"Bitch," I heard Commandress Roseanne mutter, under her breath.

I managed to shuffle over to the adjacent household, and reached communication distance with Stud Longun.

"What are we gonna do?" asked Longun.

I looked behind us at the Dileag skyline, and up at its highest building, an oval-shaped skyscraper which towered above all others, culminating in a standard tit and nipple design at its peak, and I answered:

"Reach for the sky."

*

The menfolk of Commandress Roseanne's household crowded around the television.

This was a proud moment for the "family," as our Commandress was to appear in a live interview on television alongside Chief Delegate from the Amazons, Queen Iyana, and to mark the occasion, Chef Niko had caught and fried a rat, and presented it on some crackers.

As Niko shared round his 'Rat-Snack Crackers," we watched as

Commandress Roseanne took her position, tense shouldered, alongside the elegant Iyana on a sofa.

The host, a non-binary, fix smiled, hateful-eyed, screeching thing named O.P introduced the show to the studio guests.

"We have an amazing show for you today. Coming up, the chocolate that makes you thin. But first, representing a trade delegation, leader of the Amazon Women from the Amazon, live on Daytime TV, it's the beautiful Queen Iyana, and the Commandress who invited her here, Commandress Roseanne."

The audience could be heard applauding as O.P took a position opposite the two guests.

Commandress Roseanne shifted uncomfortably on the sofa while Queen Iyana sat upright and composed.

"Now, you two have only met via tele-screen before, right Commandress Roseanne? But you'll be giving the outsiders a tour later..." began O.P.

Iyana interjected immediately.

"Outsiders. I don't like that term. My people come from the Ungari tribe. It means "Women on Top.""

"The ugly tribe?" asked Commandress Roseanne, causing a faint gasp from the television audience, and the nervous munching of Rat-Snack Crackers from at least some of the audience at home.

Iyana glared at Commandress Roseanne with a look of utter contempt.

O.P intervened:

"Right, right. Sorry. "Outsider" is such a man's word. But you two are friends, right?"

Commandress Roseanne then, curiously, chose to affect the speech of a 15-year-old West Coast schoolgirl.

"Totally, we get on really well. We're friends. I don't care if, like, they're different. I'm cool with it. We can hang out."

"Queen Iyana, what do you notice about Dileag that's different?" asked O.P.

"Interesting. Firstly, the women here are much rounder."

Commandress Roseanne and O.P simultaneously threw back their heads and squeezed forth some fake laughter, diffusing the tension.

Before O.P could stop her, Commandress Roseanne entered the fray with:

"She is super cool. Totally says what she thinks. That's an

awesome skirt. I haven't seen anything like that before. Did you make it yourself? Where do you buy your tan?"

"Maybe we should let Queen Iyana ask a question," intervened O.P.

"It's ok, if the Commandress has anything to ask," Iyana parried.

"Yes, I do have a question, as a matter of fact. Regarding this trade agreement," Commandress Roseanne began. "Do you sell cakes?

"I notice there seems to be an absence of children on this planet," Iyana stated, maintaining firm eye contact on Commandress Roseanne, who bounced nervously on the sofa.

"We have a saying, "children are best not seen, but not heard."

"And men?"

"Oh, we have men, lots of men. I myself have the finest specimen of manhood in all Dileag," lied the Commandress.

"Well, where is he?"

I didn't hear the rest of the interview. I had to pop out to get the hang-gliders.

CHAPTER FIFTEEN

REACH FOR THE SKY

The hang-gliders, retrieved from storage in the sports centre and tucked into our backpacks, created an uncomfortable weight on our shoulders, although Stud Longun and Stud Mastall seemed to carry the extra kilos more easily than I.

We entered the skyscraper, the tallest building in Dileag, at lobby level: I, followed by Longun and Mastall, with the short, excited steps of someone who was both very excited, and very, very short.

We knew that we couldn't get through the wall, and we'd already failed in trying to get under it, but if we could manage to get over it.

That was the extent of the plan, and its shortcomings were made clear when we came across a security desk, and a frowning female security officer, who fixed us with a penetrating stare under which we stared back with slack-jawed dumbfoundedness.

The lobby was a hive of activity, with important looking ladies in power suits darting to and fro, hot beverages in hand, and massive high heels under foot.

It wasn't clear what these ladies actually did in the building, but trying to outdo each other in the height of their heels seemed to be part of it.

The heels had reached an average of 20 inches each, and caused the majority of ladies to stumble at least once as she made her way across the lobby.

It was one such lady who stumbled into the back of Stud Mastall, causing the various parts of his hang-glider to spill from his backpack and clatter on the floor.

"Oh," said the security officer. "You're the plumbers!"

I looked to Stud Longun and Stud Mastall. They looked at each-other and back at me. They were still slack jawed and dumbfounded. I had to think fast, and I answered with:

"Yes, we are the plumbers."

"Good, we've been waiting years to get that fixed. The tank's out the back."

*

The climb to the top of the building, via the maintenance stairway, was long and arduous. Thankfully, Stud Longun carried my backpack for me, so we made good time.

Perched atop the dome-like teet, we unfolded our hang-gliders - wing-like contraptions operated through a harness - the strong breeze at altitude filling our lungs with air and our minds with confidence.

The city lay out before us: the business district, the malls, the sports stadium, the roads, the wall, and beyond, beckoning...

"Right, Studs, let's give this a try," I said, mad on oxygen. "Do as I do."

I keeled over and threw up, having made the fateful error, mid-sentence, of looking down.

"Maybe we should try a different approach," suggested Stud Longun.

"I'm thinking violence," offered Stud Mastall.

Dizzy, I wiped my face with my red tunic, trying to re-orientate myself, and trying not to have vomit on my face.

"You know, I impregnated a Commandress once?" Stud Mastall continued, out of nowhere. "They reassign you immediately so you don't form a bond with the child. I never got to see my kid. I never even got to see my pointy hat."

I turned to face the skies, spread the wings of the hang-glider above me, and ran off the tit.

The leap was not just for my own freedom. It was in honour of all the Studs who had never seen the children they had fathered; it was for all the Duds who were right now having their faces melted off by nuclear waste; it was for all the nameless husbands who were treated as part of the furniture.

And as the wings caught the current and I took flight, I could hear the cheers of the two Studs behind me celebrating our triumph. It was for all of us.

It was then that a slight change in the direction of the wind caught the wings at an angle, inflated my tunic - raised it to the waist, spun me around and sent me back in the direction of the skyscraper.

Even from a distance I could see the looks of confusion etched into the faces of the two Studs.

Spread-eagled, I slammed into the window of one of the offices of the skyscraper with a splat, my testicles firmly pressed against the glass.

My appearance interrupted a meeting of lady execs on the other side of the glass. The attention of the executives turned away from a presentation, upon which, ironically, was displayed an image of a penis, towards my own form, as I slowly slid down the side of the slightly concave building.

*

The whole thing caused quite a commotion in the lobby of the skyscraper.

Commandress Roseanne was halfway through giving Queen Iyana a tour of the underground schools when she was alerted to the news that her Stud was found plastered to the side of Dileag's largest skyscraper with a pair of wings on his back.

The news had come at an unfortunate time, since Commandress Roseanne and Iyana were said to be listening to a fascinating lecture by the academic Professor Jane Masterson, who was providing evidence for her theory that every male character who had ever appeared in literature of any kind, was a closet homosexual.

I and the two Studs were rounded up and presented to the Commandress, who had rushed over to the skyscraper as soon as she'd heard, accompanied by Iyana and Iyana's closest aids.

We were surrounded by business ladies who had interrupted their penis presentations to come down and witness the confrontation, as well as lady CEOs of companies which occupied the building, and the security staff.

"Why did you let them in?" Commandress Roseanne demanded of the female security guard.

"I thought they were plumbers," pleaded the security guard.

"Plumbers!" screamed Roseanne. "We had all the plumbers killed three years ago when it was found that they were all men!"

"Ah, that explains it," said the security guard.

"This security guard does not display the competencies for her position," observed the Commandress, quite rightly, to the Chief of Security. "Remove her from her position immediately, and give her a place on the Board of Directors so she can keep out of trouble."

"Is it acceptable here for one's menfolk to climb up the side of buildings?" Queen Iyana asked, treating this like it was all part of the tour.

Commandress Roseanne had seemingly delayed turning her attention to me, and I soon picked up why.

"You're hilarious, so hilarious," she told Iyana, and then to me, and with a slightly girlish tone: "So, Stud Ramrod, why were you stuck to the side of this building, dressed like a bat?"

I picked up on a curious dynamic.

Although, no doubt, furious with me, Commandress Roseanne was also deeply embarrassed that all this was playing out in front of Queen Iyana. It was those feelings of embarrassment which the Commandress tended to in the moment.

I bundled the advantage and came out with:

"We were making a statement about men's rights."

This, of course, drew a gasp of horror from the crowd, but I recovered with:

"We were making a statement that men's rights shouldn't be treated seriously."

A collective sigh of approval from the crowd merged with one of relief from myself and the two Studs.

"See, boys will be boys? We like them to be active. It's good for the sperm count," Commandress Roseanne chimed in.

"And this one has yet to impregnate you?" Queen Iyana observed.

"Not yet, but he will. He will."

I looked over to the two Studs and gave a comforting wink.

We had survived another day.

And with that, Commandress Roseanne leaned forward and attached an explosive electronic tag to my testicles, and then we all went home.

CHAPTER SIXTEEN

TO DIE OR TO DANCE

I awoke in the middle of the night to find Commandress Roseanne sitting at the end of my bed, staring at me with a look of calm malevolence.

"I was just trying to decide whether to kill you in your sleep, or to castrate you," said the lady.

"And which of those did you go with?" I had to ask.

"I dreamt that you were having sex with another woman."

"I have an electric clamp on my penis."

If it wasn't slap bang in the middle of my primetime-sleep-hours, I'm sure the conversation would have been fascinating.

"You know, I could have you executed for what you did today?" she observed, as I momentarily drifted back off to sleep. "If I didn't have to save face in front of the Amazons... Sometimes I feel like you don't love me."

I digested this last statement like a morsel of fatty meat in my mouth, impossible to respond to, too stubborn to deal with.

"You never buy me flowers," the Commandress continued.

"I have to follow a prescribed shopping list."

Commandress Roseanne held up a ludicrous, bright white tuxedo; one that would only be seen on a total ponce...

"Put this on. We're going to a nightclub."

*

81

A horrific noise from the nightclub spilled out onto the street as a busty bouncer opened the door to Commandress Roseanne, Queen Iyana, the Amazon entourage, and me in the bright, white tux.

"Only people at the very top know about this place. We converted the post office," the Commandress wailed to Iyana as we entered the hell-hole.

"No wonder my letters always went missing," I added, but the ladies didn't seem to hear me, because not one showed any appreciation for the quip.

Commandress Roseanne punched the air and let out a strange whooping sound as she led us deeper into the pit of the dark-space, while Iyana followed in a state of detached observation, and I tried to remain anonymous despite my glow of fluorescent white.

It's hard to make sense of what I saw before me, because fundamentally the place had been designed to encourage patrons to lose sense: brain mashing music, a formless queue for the bar, idiots gyrating on the dance-floor, lighting designed with the impossible task of flattering the patrons.

"Isn't it wonderful?" Commandress Roseanne guffawed.

In the shadows, other Commandresses sat in booths with their obedient Studs, snorting powder off outstretched Stud legs, grinding up against Studs on the dance-floor, telling their life stories to desperate Studs in quiet corners, amongst undelivered parcels from amazon.com.

"Let's do shots!" Commandress Roseanne shouted, dragging me over to the bar, where the Commandress licked some salt, drank a small vestibule of liquid, and bit a lemon, while Iyana and her entourage looked on with suitable bafflement.

Commandress Roseanne then pulled back my head and poured the same toxic liquid down my gullet, ensuring the rest of the evening would remain a blur.

At one point we ran into the wart-ridden Commandress Rita with poor Stud Longun at her side. The two Commandresses seemed to have a conversation, bellowing the word "Wallarallaralla," into each other's ears, while Stud Longun looked to the ground, embarrassed, and I chimed in with "I quite agree," whenever the Commandresses looked my way.

Then we were all in a booth: Commandress Rita with her tongue down the throat of Stud Longun, me crippled with Commandress Roseanne on my lap, and Iyana by the side, watched over by her entourage.

"My first husband, he never gave me the attention I deserve," the Commandress bellowed into my ear. "He never appreciated me; if I saw him today, he'd be beheaded."

I'd handed her a package I'd found under the table.

"I think I ordered this one. It's a mini-grill."

"You know, if your Stud fails to impregnate you, I will take him," Iyana interjected, presumably out of boredom.

"You'll what?" screamed Commandress Roseanne.

"I'll take him for myself."

This got everyone's attention.

"Why would you want to take him?" Commandress Roseanne, for once, spoke for all of us.

"He has a high threshold for suffering. That's attractive to someone who likes a challenge. Plus, he's incredibly tolerant."

Iyana had a point.

"He's lucky to have me," burped the Commandress. "You hear? He's lucky to have me!"

"Don't raise your voice at an Amazon."

"Oh, yeah. What are you going to do about it?"

"I'm going to declare war."

"Good. Let's have a war then!"

This had escalated quickly.

I interjected with the ineffective:

"Um, I'm not sure if that's…"

"We gonna kick yo' ass!" Commandress Roseanne screamed. "We're at war!"

Commandress Rita let out one of those "whooop" sounds, and then this whoop sound merged with the ludicrous lyric, "Crazy in Love," hollered from the loudspeaker, and this generated more whoops and fake joy, and within seconds, the Commandresses had dragged Longun and I to the dance-floor and were bumping their fat asses into our bodies, totally oblivious to the fact they had just entered a war.

*

"Loosen up!" Commandress Roseanne screamed into my ear as she groped me on the dance-floor.

"I'm slightly worried about the war," I explained.

"Promise you'll never leave me," ordered the Commandress.

"What?"

"I'll never let you go," she screamed.

"Never?"

"I have a surprise for you!"

And with that, she pulled me off the dance-floor and dragged me up a flight of stairs to a VIP upper deck, reserved for the very top echelon of asshole.

"I know how it's every Stud's dream to have two women at once," the Commandress announced, in her usual confusing fashion.

She pushed open the door to the VIP room to reveal Commandress Rita draped over a heart-shaped bed, waiting expectantly.

Commandress Roseanne sallied over to Commandress Rita and joined her on the bed.

The two Commandresses looked over to me expectantly.

And not for the first time that week, I keeled over and threw up on the floor.

CHAPTER SEVENTEEN

NICOLETTE

I sat next to Commandress Roseanne in the back of the limo as we pulled away from the nightclub, embarrassed at having vomited at the thought of a threesome with two Commandresses, and still rather perturbed by the fact that we were now at war.

There's an awkwardness that exists between a man and woman when the man has just thrown up at the sight of the woman laid out on a heart-shaped bed, and I tried to diffuse this awkwardness by whistling a nice little tune I made up on the spot.

Commandress Roseanne conveyed her appreciation by slapping me hard across the face and sending my glasses flying.

Nicolette, respecting the sensitivities between myself and the Commandress, closed the partition between the front and back of the limo.

I thanked Nicolette, just as the partition fully closed, sealing me in with the Commandress at the back of the car.

"You like her, don't you?" Commandress Roseanne asked, somewhat surprisingly.

"Nicolette? She's very kind. Everyone here is, really."

"I want you to fuck her for me," said the Commandress, even more surprisingly.

"I'm infertile, Ramrod, it's clear. Three Studs now, and nothing. I was infertile before the war; I'm sure infertile now."

I sat dumbfounded.

"There's social status to be had in producing a child. It's the only way to reach a higher rank. If you and Nicolette fathered a child, for me, it would benefit us all."

I gulped.

"You're a perverse little bastard, Stud Ramrod. Nicolette was a gymnast. I doubt you'll need any medical stimulus."

*

I knocked on the door of Nicolette's quarters, above the garage, feeling out of place standing there in my tunic and fake moustache.

I felt even more out of place when Nicolette answered dressed in all-black lingerie, the moonlight casting a halo around her young, fit body.

"This is pretty awkward," I said, trying to ease the situation and feeling sorry for the poor girl.

Nicolette yanked me inside, threw me on the bed, and slammed the door behind us.

Immediately, I picked up a dripping sound coming from Nicolette's en-suite bathroom.

"You've got a leaky tap," I observed, as Nicolette backflipped in the air and landed down on top of me.

"It's been like that for ages," she said. "Since the plumbers died."

"It must be very annoying," I said, as Nicolette contorted her limbs like a compressed time-bomb and then exploded into action. "I'm terribly audio-sensitive."

"How unfortunate for you," said Nicolette, as she writhed her body upon me like a cheetah devouring its prey.

"Unfortunate for all of us," I agreed. "A plumber is an adventurer who traces leaky pipes to their source."

"What's that?" Nicolette asked, while upside down.

"It's a quote," I explained, and then I gave her: "The society which scorns excellence in plumbing as a humble activity and tolerates shoddiness in philosophy because it is an exalted activity will have neither good plumbing nor good philosophy: neither its pipes nor its theories will hold water."

Nicolette, sweating now, seemed to approve, and so I continued with: "A guy digging ditches or a plumber wiping joints - it solves problems, you know? You have to dig this hole so wide, so long, so deep. You dig it, and that's it - Lee Marvin."

Nicolette cried out in agreement, and performed an advanced back-flip.

When I regained consciousness, I found Nicolette lying in my arms, a slight look of disappointment on her face, understandably so - our conversation had been cut short.

"It's ok, it happens to lots of guys when I do the Produnova vault," Nicolette suggested.

"The blood must have rushed away from my brain," I explained. "It's a shame, though, I was just about to mention Alan Rudolph - You take plumbing and woman's nature: they're both unpredictable and filled with hidden mysteries. All man can do is serve them properly so they flow the way they're designed to."

*

"So I was stuck in that position for three weeks," Nicolette was saying as we entered the mansion looking for a midnight snack.

It turned out, though, that we didn't get a midnight snack. Instead, we were confronted by Commandress Roseanne standing in the lobby, flanked by It, Marku and Niko, and opposite them, Uncle Joe.

Beside Uncle Joe stood someone who was instantly recognizable and yet who appeared as though from another time - the giant from the Gonad Assessment Centre whose results had presumably been mixed up with mine - the actual Stud Ramrod.

"Who's this?" asked Nicolette.

"This is Stud Ramrod. The real Stud Ramrod," announced Commandress Roseanne.

"Well then who is this?" asked Nicolette, stepping away from me.

"This is Dud Wimpole," Commandress Roseanne explained. "Dud Wimpole is an idiot."

"There's been a terrible mix up at the testing centre and I'm afraid we've all lost face," Uncle Joe interjected. "It was ordered that we retest this man after he was spotted on the nuclear waste site singing the theme tune to 'Oklahoma.' He is the real Stud Ramrod."

"I eat nuclear waste for breakfast," the real Stud Ramrod boasted - figuratively, I hope.

"Shall we lock up the imposter?" suggested the sneering It.

"We can't lock him up," growled the Commandress. "We've

already introduced him to the visitors as Stud Ramrod. We can't be made to look weak as we go into war."

"War, Commandress?" Uncle Joe asked.

"We went out. Shots were taken. Things were said. We're going to war."

"Yes, Commandress," Uncle Joe nodded.

"Nicolette, you will try to conceive with the real Stud Ramrod." Commandress Roseanne ordered, causing Nicolette to reluctantly skip over to the visitor and fling her arms around his shoulders. "Meanwhile, we will prepare for war. The Amazons are a peace-loving nation, as are we. They will elect only one warrior to fight on their behalf - a fight to the death."

"And who will we elect in this fight to the death?" asked It, loving every minute of this.

Commandress Roseanne pointed my way and announced, of course:

"Dud Fucking Wimpole!"

PART THREE

WAR

CHAPTER EIGHTEEN

THE PLAN

Who am I?

In recounting these events, I've repeatedly had to ask myself that question.

I was no victim. I'd had choices along the way, decisions to make. I could have come clean. I could have gone clean - nuclear waste, that is

My present position was in part my doing. How then, and why, had I cultivated a place for myself in the world that was the direct opposite of where I would logically want to be?

How and why had I made a series of choices, taken a series of actions, that had first positioned me as a virile impregnator of ladies, and then as a one-man warlord, neither of which were suitable for a man of a slightly nervous disposition?

Should an individual be judged by his words or his actions? I tried to describe myself at the start of this narrative as I honestly saw myself - as a harm avoiding, peace-loving, space-needing, impotent, yet content individual, unburdened by ambition.

But if I was to be judged by my actions alone, well that would point towards me being a sexually perverse, hyper masochistic, war-mongering, daredevil revolutionary with a total disregard for his own limitations.

Why the discrepancy?

The answers to this are still not clear to me. I guess we make choices which appear to make most sense to us at the time, but this sense is often clouded by fear, delusion, anxiety, medication, ego, genetics, desperation…

Try as I might, it's all difficult to unravel, and it's futile to pretend that there was any consistency in my decision making, any rationality in my thought process, anything resembling consistency of character. Heck, I didn't even have consistency of name, although now, at least, there seemed to be common agreement - I was Dud Wimpole.

These were the thoughts that filled my mind as I sat at breakfast with the rest of the household, watching the news the next morning - bar Commandress Roseanne, whose Women's Wrath had kicked in and who was out chasing chickens in the yard and tearing them apart with her bare teeth.

I considered myself lucky. I could have been one of those chickens, having failed to impregnate the Commandress ahead of her Magic Lady Time, but I had been spared to face a far more brutal slaughter on behalf of the entire lady-folk of Dileag, in a figurative war against the Amazons.

It would be a fitting and unsurprising end, and the news people were excitedly reporting on the build-up now.

"War," the news announcer declared, grinning. "Dileag is at war with the Amazons today because they are real bitches!"

"Pass the waffles, please," Nicolette requested, perched atop of Stud Ramrod's knee.

Ramrod had made a sumptuous breakfast (It was consoling the now usurped Niko in the kitchen) and managed to fix a leaky tap at the same time, and so had gained some favour with the household. "Stud Ramrod has a tattoo of a dragon on his penis," Nicolette added, somewhat unnecessarily.

Commandress Roseanne appeared on the screen in a pre-recorded interview:

"I did the only thing any self-respecting woman would do. I declared war. As in any civilised society, war will not be settled by armies of women going away to fight. Instead, our battle will be fought by men. The visitors will choose their finest specimen, and we will choose ours, and they will fight to the death. For us, this warrior will be the mighty Stud Ramrod."

A particularly unflattering picture of myself being clamped at the balls following the hang-gliding escapade appeared on the screen, with a caption: "Our finest specimen."

"You will be pulled limb from limb," observed Marku. "Honey."

At this point, Marku was asking for someone to pass him the honey. He was not, and I would like to be clear on this point, referring to me as Honey.

"We'll be bringing you live coverage of the Stud Ramrod send-off parade this weekend, as well as the war itself" continued the excited news announcer. "But first up, headlines: the moon's in Scorpio today, which is good news for Geminis…"

I considered pleading with Commandress Roseanne that it would be better for Dileag's morale if we didn't send a warrior who was guaranteed to fail spectacularly, but her hatred of me seemed to override her loyalty to Dileag, and besides, it's difficult to bargain with a woman with chicken blood on her face, so I didn't bother trying.

Instead, I came up with a brilliant plan.

*

"Not to worry, lads, everything's going to be fine," I told the slightly despondent Stud Longun and Stud Mastall at an impromptu gathering in the sports centre locker room, mid-shopping trip.

The stadium itself was being prepared for the evening's "war," with a steel cage ring being erected centre position and seating arranged for a stage and opening ceremony. We had been lucky to escape detection, particularly with the two Studs dragging their heels, lacking the hopeful bounce in their steps they had previously been blessed with.

"But I don't understand how you fighting to the death is a good thing," Stud Longun, declared, really setting me up nicely to announce my remarkable plan. "You're a lover, not a fighter."

It would have detracted from the moment at that point to explain that I was also not "a lover."

"You know, I heard this whole women on top thing was started off by a bunch of men," Stud Mastall chimed in, unusually morose. "I heard that men were tired of doing all the work, fighting all the wars, never seeing their kids, so a group of guys put on some drag and some lady pseudonyms, and they did marches, and wrote books, about how women were victims not to be working, and warring, and apparently the women actually bought it."

"That's very helpful, Stud Mastall, thank you," I said, trying to return the poor chap from speculative fantasies to more urgent matters, but he continued:

"Except when the women got into those positions of work, and war, and isolation from their homes and families, they realised they'd been duped, and the hatred this generated for the men, and for themselves, boiled over. It's a hatred that now dominates the world."

"Don't worry, we're going to change all that," I told the two Studs.

"How?" asked Longun.

"Let me tell you my brilliant plan…" I began.

Unfortunately, I was interrupted by the sound of footsteps coming down the players' tunnel and the arrival of Stud Ramrod, It, Marku and Niko, and so the whole thing was ruined.

*

"Nice little pad, you have here, Dud Wimpole" Stud Ramrod bellowed, standing proud, hands on hips.

"Who's Dud Wimpole?" asked Stud Longun.

"Long story," I said.

"We followed you," Marku added, reliably stating the obvious.

"In trouble now, aren't you, Dud Wimpole?" sneered It.

"Who?" asked Stud Longun.

The two parties eyed each other like two rival packs of wolves, I and Studs Longun and Mastall on one side, Ramrod and the household of It, Marku and Niko on the other.

Stud Mastall spoke first.

"We have a plan. We're going to change everything - this whole society."

The rival gang let out a cheer.

"We're all for that. Let's rip this hell-hole apart. What's the plan?" asked Stud Ramrod, quite flatteringly, needing my input.

The rival gang was on board.

"Well, it's like this," I began. "A few years ago, all the plumbers of Dileag were executed when it was found that the whole profession was being occupied by men. Now, there are leaking taps everywhere, septic tanks overflowing, piping, no doubt, fit to burst. The women don't know how to plumb. When a washer goes, a household usually moves."

I waited, allowing this to set in, and for at least one of the group to guess the next bit.

They didn't, so I continued.

"We need to show the importance of men to this society, beyond the roles of just Stud or Dud. While I'm being paraded, you guys sneak away and fix Dileag's plumbing. I'll announce at the sending-off ceremony, prior to the planned fight to the death, what you have done, proving our value, and stating that unless the women want leaky taps and non-flushing toilets, they need to release me and give greater rights to men!"

It's fair to say that a mightily triumphant roar echoed off of the walls of that men's locker room. Much pats on the back were had. Handshakes were exchanged. Cheers and songs of joy were shared.

Even the otherwise morose Niko, having been usurped as the family's finest chef, joined in the celebrations. I'm proud to reflect that it was a moment of joyous optimism for us all.

In the end, the men ignored the plan entirely, and while I was sent off to fight to the death, they stole a stock of unused fighter planes, flew over Dileag, and blew up the city and everything with it.*

*spoiler alert

CHAPTER NINETEEN

THE PARADE

So, here's how the disaster unfolded.

It was a beautiful and calm weekend morning. The sun sent beams of golden light through the powder white clouds as though beckoning in a new era. A cool breeze drifted towards the north.

Humidity, if I was absolutely forced to take a guess, was probably around 65%.

The crowds gathered on the streets of Dileag from Commandress Roseanne's mansion, to the stadium itself, where I would be presented on stage, ahead of the fight to the death.

It was a proper, and if I'm to be honest, quite moving, send-off.

Each of the warring parties had a float: the Commandresses, with Roseanne taking pride of place on a throne, which I and the men of the house had been up all night making out of paper mache, and me at her feet, sitting cross-legged, patiently, while waving at the crowd.

The Amazons had their own float, too, following behind ours. Theirs was made from bamboo, and floated slightly above the ground on some kind of hover modifications, but they were just showing off.

As I waved at the crowds, and they waved back using what must have been a customary single-digit salute, a feeling of pride filled my body. I had explained my plan in the minutest detail, gained the unanimous agreement and praise in its excellence from all, and had shielded myself from the possibility that if it wasn't executed perfectly, I would be ripped to bits.

And there were the Studs, now, waving from the crowds in a glowing huddle: Stud Longun, Stud Mastall, Marku, Niko, It and of course, Stud Ramrod. They were all in on it. I gave them a knowing wink and Ramrod gave me a wink back.

Right on cue, they backed away into the crowd and were lost from sight, to go, as I was still fully expecting, to fix the faulty plumbing of Dileag.

Ramrod, however, had got wind of there being a store of unused fighter jets on the outskirts of the city, parked in hangers following the female declaration of sweetness and peace, and forgotten about.

The sweet and peaceful ones had even left the things fully armed, not to be troubled by matters such as practicality, and so the merry band of bastards were able to sneak into the hangers, steal the planes, and take to the skies, and it was to the hangers that they were now headed, while the eyes of the city were watching my death march.

I even had the naiveté to give a tearful salute to the spot where the Studs had been standing, which generated even more single finger waves from some elderly ladies who had filled the space.

Still, none of this should detract from the fact that this was a moment of pride for me, fuelled, though it was, by delusion and the total ignorance of what was about to happen.

And when I saw a group of young girls hold aloft and wave bespectacled action figures in my likeness, I couldn't help myself but stand up and wave back, until Commandress Roseanne shot a foot up into my bollocks causing me to sit down again.

And when the girls took out pins and started poking the figures of me with them, which in retrospect were most likely voodoo effigies, I was thankfully in too much gonadal agony to care.

*

The stadium was packed to the rafters with fans gathered to watch the war.

A steel-cage wrestling ring took pride of place in the centre of the stadium, but for now, all eyes were on the stage, at the far end, where I was to be presented to the crowd.

I waited back-stage with Uncle Joe by my side, anticipating my big moment.

I peaked round some scaffolding to get sight of the front rows. Amazons and Commandresses sat either side of a central aisle.

Where were the Studs, though? The plan had been for them to join the seating reserved for the household of the Commandress upon return from their plumbing heroics, and in time for me to introduce them triumphantly to the crowd.

Had they been delayed? I asked myself, still not getting it. Had they ran out of washers?

Commandress Roseanne took to the stage and bowed to the Head Brain - the pickled organ of former pop star Madonna - and then stepped up to a standing microphone to address the crowd.

"Ladies, and ladies, I have a message from the Head Brain," announced Commandress Roseanne, and then reading from a note: "When I envisioned this society, little could I have imagined a prouder day: a man sent to his almost certain death in the name of female bickering." The crowd went wild. "Because that's how important our whims are!"

Hysterical, really.

"If Stud Ramrod wins the fight," Commandress Roseanne continued - her own words, now. "We win the argument between our two societies, whatever that may have been about. If he loses, we get to enjoy the spectacle of a bloodbath." The crowd was loving this. Still no sign of the Studs, though. "And now I welcome to the stage to say a few words, Uncle Joe, with Stud Ramrod."

This was my moment. I had planned there and then to introduce the Studs and the menfolk of Commandress Roseanne's house, share the news of their plumbing good deeds, and announce that if, as a gender, men were not taken more seriously with immediate effect, the whole of Dileag would go back to leaky pipes forever more.

In the absence of the Studs ahead of their big moment, I resolved to go ahead anyway, and announce their great feats while they were probably still mopping up after a good day's work.

I stepped up to the microphone.

"Go check your taps..." was all I managed to say, before Uncle Joe put a hand on my shoulder and whispered in my ear that it was he who was to share a few words, and not me. The glare from Commandress Roseanne confirmed this to be the case.

"I present to you, Stud Ramrod," Uncle Joe began. "The finest specimen of manhood in Dileag. Not only is he Dileag's greatest and most virile carrier of sperm; Stud Ramrod is our greatest and most vicious fighter-warrior and tonight, he will fight for your victory, or he will die trying!"

That was it, then. "Go check your taps," was all I managed.

And I was sent to the ring, for a fight to the death, hoping, at least, that "Go check your taps" was taken as an intriguing suggestion which would lead the people of Dileag to investigate their plumbing, and to see and appreciate the good work the men had done, and not, simply, as the strange and final cry of a madman.

*

It was time for the main event. Dusk had fallen, and the stadium was lit with neon, a spot-light beaming down on to the steel cage ring.

Commandress Roseanne had taken her seat, flanked by Commandress Rita and Nicolette on one side of the ring.

On the other side sat Queen Iyana and her Amazons, poised and regal, and yet, united with the 80,000 or so other spectators in the stadium in a sense of excited anticipation.

An announcer took to the ring:

"Ladies, and ladies, we have a 12 round bout to the death, for the dignity of our people, to settle our war, and to sleep with Queen Iyana. First into the ring, the challenger, with a record of no fights, no wins and facing certain death, the twerp, Stud Ramrod."

The crowd exhaled a roar of pent up aggression. The waiting was over. The fight was now. And still the Studs hadn't turned up with evidence of their plumbing.

I began the long walk up the aisle, led by Uncle Joe, from the stage end of the stadium towards the ring, as lights flashed in my eyes and people threw popcorn in my face.

To make matters worse, a mad singer bellowed from the loudspeaker, the lyric "We run the world girls, we run the run world girls," as if this observation wasn't obvious enough.

"Who run this mutha? Girls. Who run this mutha? Girls," were the lyrics. Utterly mental.

Amid this, Uncle Joe shouted unhelpful phrases such as "lead with the jab," "use the ropes," and "stay on the back foot," all of which had no meaning to me whatsoever.

I did understand him when he also suggested I "remember the training," at which point I shouted back, reminding him that we hadn't covered this in the training.

It was when we reached the ring, pasted in soft drinks and snacks thrown from the crowd, that I realised, conclusively, that the whole plumbing thing was off.

At that moment, as I climbed the steps in the corner, Uncle Joe decided to call me back with some final information.

"Dud," he said. "Dud, I have to tell you something. I realise, now, that I've started to identify as a woman."

"Now's probably not the time, Uncle Joe," I called back, perhaps unkindly, but I was about to be murdered.

"Please," said Uncle Joe. "Call me Auntie Joe."

I entered the ring, where the announcer prepared to introduce my opponent.

I pulled back my hood, and started to skip from side to side with nervous anticipation, throwing a few punches in the air as a show of goodwill.

You see, I was pretty happy with myself in that moment, because somehow, on the way up the steps into the ring, I had come up with a second brilliant plan.

The new plan would have me pointing out to my opponent that we had far more in common than we had in opposition.

If I could just avoid being killed outright in the opening seconds of the bout, I would make the observation that a system which requires one gender to shed its time, its blood, its life for the benefit of the other, was inherently corrupt. I would point out that as men, we shared the common ground of being treated as brutes, seen as brutes and the condemnation to act as brutes.

I would appeal to his kindness, his compassion and his decency as a man.

It turned out, though, that my opponent was a woman, so I was doomed.

CHAPTER TWENTY

THE FIGHT

"And now, welcome to the ring, his opponent," bellowed the announcer into the microphone. "Weighing 900 pounds and representing the Amazon Women from the Amazon, the undefeated, the unstable, Lady God Wartoff!"

The lady in question, a 7 foot tall, female hulk, shaven-headed, face tattooed, dressed in a Gladiator costume with spikes protruding in every direction entered the arena, sending the crowd mad with blood-lust: females shaking, crying, wetting themselves.

"And your referee, Babs Johnston," concluded the announcer, before leaving the ring and making way for Lady God Wartoff.

Referee Babs locked me in the steel cage prison with Wartoff, and went back to playing with her phone from a safe distance in the front row.

"It's a pleasure to meet you," I said to the Lady, who in response snorted through her nose and spat on the ring. I noticed, too, that she hadn't bothered to remove her spikes, as the bell sounded for the start of round one.

We were off.

The opening seconds of the match were even: two warriors circling each other, sizing each other up, looking for an opening. Then, Lady God Wartoff got bored, picked me up, and threw me against the cage.

The crowd groaned. They had wanted blood. The fight looked to be over already.

Somehow, I made it to my feet. This immediately proved to be a bad idea, as the Lady God came at me, arms outstretched, gnashing her teeth.

I countered brilliantly by running away; except there was nowhere to go; so what ensued was the no doubt odd sight of Lady God Wartoff chasing me around the ring in circles, and then back the other way, until Wartoff managed to grab me by the arm, swing me around, and throw me into my corner.

Uncle Joe clambered to my side, shouting at me through from the other side of the steel cage.

"Listen, you're going to have to use your skills," said the delusional Uncle.

"I haven't got any skills," I gasped, winded to the core.

"You're going to have to seduce her," screamed the confused maniac.

"She's gay, isn't she?" I had to assume.

"Use your training, get out there, seduce her."

*

Lady God Wartoff waited for me in the centre of the ring, snorting like a bull in heat.

The Stud training had focused on techniques to satisfy and seduce females. Now it, and I, would be put to the ultimate test.

I walked around Wartoff, circling the giant, while adopting the seductive, jerking motion of a pigeon. This created visible curiosity in the face of the monster, and the jeers of the crowd morphed into a collectively confused murmur.

This had bought me some time. So far, not so bad. I added on a little head wobbling.

It was time to step things up. I would try a flirtatious compliment.

I hit her with:

"Do you mind if I stare at you up close instead of from across the ring?"

The Lady God looked stunned, so I quickly followed this with a:

"Shall we talk, now, or continue flirting from a distance?"

The Lady God slapped me hard across the face.

This sent me down to my knees, and the crowd back into a frenzy.

The inevitability of gruesome death was back on.

While still down, I screamed up at the Lady God:

"Is it hot in here, or is it just you?"

"What?" bellowed Wartoff.

I then caught her with:

"If I said that you have a nice body, would you hold it against me?"

Lady God Wartoff chopped me hard across the chest and the crowd roared its approval.

I'd never been chopped before. I doubt many people have. Let me tell you, it hurts.

The blow spun me around, and had me land face-first on the mat.

"Remember the negs!" Uncle Joe screamed from the corner.

I'd never met the Negs.

I assumed Uncle Joe had lost it like the rest of the crowd.

To my left, Queen Iyana looked on with an expression of detached curiosity, stroking her spear with casual abandon.

To my right, Commandress Roseanne stood up and screamed out words of encouragement such as:

"Stop embarrassing me," and "typical man!"

I pulled myself to my feet to give it one last go.

"Apart from being beautiful" I began, coughing up a lung full of blood in the process, "what do you do for a living?"

The Lady God roared to the sky, pumping her arms up and down as though channeling energy from the cosmos.

So I caught her with:

"Is there a rainbow, because you're the treasure I've been searching for?"

Lady God Wartoff picked me up above her head, much to the delight of the voracious crowd. She then spun me around like a helicopter and sent me flying into the air. I landed with a splat on the mat, finished.

Lady God Wartoff turned me onto my back using her toe and stood over me, erect, with a foot on my chest, posing for the crowd.

I was done. The war was over. The crowd was going mental.

The Lady God wasn't quite ready to call it a night, though. She went over to the corner of the ring and started to scale the steel-cage.

By the time she reached the top, perched on the corner of that steel frame, her head must have been 50 feet in the air. Her spikes glistened in the neon lights. Her arms outstretched, she channeled the energies of the Universe.

The crowd willed her on:

"Jump, jump, jump…"

She jumped.

*

They say that the moment before you die, your whole life flashes before your eyes. For me, that moment was when the 900 pound Lady God Wartoff, arms outstretched, spikes at all angles, flew into the air and came falling towards me, as I lay flat out in the ring.

Luckily, for me, barring perhaps the previous couple of weeks, my life had been entirely uneventful, and was easily given a run through in less than half a second.

This gave me time, miraculously, to spin out of the way just as the Lady God hit the surface, crashing headfirst, and becoming embedded, spikes down, into the mat.

The crowd was shocked. Queen Iyana put a hand to her mouth - surprised, but not displeased. Nicolette jumped wildly on her chair. Commandress Roseanne turned to face the crowd, absorbing their cheers as though they were directed to her. Uncle Joe blew me a kiss.

The crowd was even more shocked when I turned away from the inert body of Lady God Wartoff, stuck, impaled in the ring, and moved to the corner, where I then began to scale the steel cage.

That crowd wanted to see blood that night, and they didn't care whose blood. When I reached the top of the steel cage, and looked down at the now awake and struggling, but still hopelessly stuck Lady God Wartoff, both those from Dileag and those from the Amazon chanted in unison.

"Jump, jump, jump…"

It was then that the first of the fighter planes flew over the stadium, and dropped the first of its bombs on the city of Dileag. That was followed by a second plane, and a third.

Ah, so there were Stud Ramrod, Stud Longun, Stud Mastall, Marku, Niko and It, blowing everything up, I thought to myself. Inevitable.

And just as inevitably, I turned away from the ring, climbed down the other side of the steel cage, and ran away.

CHAPTER TWENTY ONE

THE FLIGHT

The sound from the fighter planes echoed through the stadium and merged with the noise of exploding bombs. The bombs created a glow that emanated in the distance from where central Dileag once stood. The city would be turned to rubble.

Stud Ramrod, Stud Longun, Stud Mastall, It, Marku and Niko had acted in the only way they knew how: they had blown everything up. They had sacrificed themselves in retaliation to a corrupt and unjust world in which they felt they had no voice. They were twits.

The last of their planes spun through the sky over the stadium and towards Dileag, performing a loop the loop, a backward spin, and a forward plummet.

Why did they believe they would be able to fly planes, anyway, without any pilot training between them?

Why had they not stuck with the plan of simply fixing the city's faulty pipes?

And what of the children in the underground schools?

They would emerge from the rubble to find a world like no other, a world of blankness and desolation, a world of no expectations and of opportunity.

I hoped that they would be able to create for themselves a better world than we had done.

The distraction created by the procession of prats in planes bought me just enough time to make it down the outside of the cage, and halfway down the aisle, before Commandress Roseanne noticed I was gone, and rising on her chair, pointed out:

"He's running away. He's emotionally abandoning me!"

80,000 people seemed to roar in agreement, including Lady God Wartoff, who managed to pull herself free from the ring mat, smash through the steel cage, and chase after me, followed by the Commandresses of Dileag, followed by the Amazons, followed by the rest of the 80,000.

I ran away faster than I had ever ran away before.

I darted into the players' tunnel.

*

The players' tunnel connected to the endless network of escalators and stairs which linked the outer floors of the stadium – concourse platforms which provided access to the seating sections, and housed filthy toilets and even filthier hot dog stands.

I sprinted up the first escalator to the ground level concourse, and was there confronted by the first of the angry thousands who flooded the outer platforms of the stadium.

Some were there from sheer panic in response to the bombing echoing over their city; some were there as part of the angry mob in direct pursuit of their warrior who had abandoned their war and their society at the most shameful time to do so; some just seemed to think we were on a break between rounds and were lining up in ill-formed queues in the rush for hot dogs and lavatories.

There was no way out on this level, the exits were blocked by the multitudes. I took to the next escalator and climbed to the next level. There, I was equally helpless.

Sprinting around the circular outer platform, I was confronted by the angry mob of Commandresses, guards at their sides, coming right for me.

"There he is!" screamed Commandress Roseanne, bounding across the concourse with all the grace of an intoxicated elephant.

I turned to go back the other way. No luck. The Amazons with their spears held aloft, and Lady God Wartoff among their number, were coming right at me.

I caught sight of a fire escape, to my right, nestled between a hot dog stand and a lavatory. Pushing through a large green door below a "no entry" sign, I found myself in a flight of unlit stairs. I headed up.

Emerging, panting, on what I expect was the seventh or eighth floor, I discovered to my satisfaction that the crowds had yet to make it on to this concourse. I let out a sigh of relief. I was free. My mind quickly envisioned a future spent alone on this concourse in happy retirement, with access to unlimited hot dogs and array of queueless lavatories.

"Not so fast," growled a familiar, slightly clichéd, voice behind me.

I turned to face Commandress Roseanne. She stood, legs apart, hands by her side, like some big, sweaty cowboy. How had she found me?

"I followed your scent," she added, apparently now reading my thoughts.

So, I legged it.

Commandress Roseanne chased me around the circular concourse, bounding high in the air with each step, displaying the uncanny agility she had exhibited at our first encounter, the mating ritual, when she had pounced high above the air before crushing me below her.

Suddenly, I could go no further. My legs spun in the air, offering no traction. Commandress Roseanne had hold of my tunic, or, more specifically, my pocket, and something in it - the book my mother had given me and that I had vowed to take everywhere with me, somewhat idiotically, it must be said, at this point.

I placed one hand on the book and turned to face Commandress Roseanne.

There we were, two titans, facing off opposite each other, each holding on to one end of "Jacqueline and the Beanstalk," neither letting go.

"You'll never be free of me," screamed the Commandress, somewhat melodramatically. "You'll never be free."

And so I let go.

Commandress Roseanne fell back, still clutching the book, landing with a splat on the concourse.

And right on cue, the stampeding hordes, led by Lady God Wartoff, made it up the escalators onto the platform, with cries of, "there he is," and "no queues!"

Sometimes it's better to be left with no choice. This is when instinct kicks in. There's less chance of screwing up that way.

Another boom from the centre of Dileag echoed across the city, and brought with it smoke into the open-air platform.

This drew me to the edge of the concourse, almost unthinking, and from there I looked down on the deserted car park below, occupied now by the empty ships of the Amazons, and the waiting limousines of the Commandresses.

And by instinct, I hiked the red tunic up above my head, ignored the screams of ladies closing in on my bare behind, and leapt off the side of the building.

Commandress Roseanne reached the edge of the concourse and could go no further.

She stood there, screaming into the night:

"He's victimising me! Dud Wimpole is victimising me!"

The tunic, acting as a hang-glider, my testicles dangling helplessly below me in the night air, took me safely down to the car park tarmac, much to the fury of my now out of reach pursuers.

I sprinted across the car park, not knowing where my legs would take me, not daring to look back.

*

My desperate run took me towards the mighty Amazon convoy ship, hovering inaccessible, 100 feet above the ground.

There, however, waiting invitingly on the tarmac, was a small landing ship, unoccupied, unguarded, unobserved.

I climbed onto the hood of the ship and pressed a release button. The hatch opened up to reveal a pilot's seat inside.

Surely not?

The control panel was simple enough: on, off, up, down. A control stick indicated forward, back - easy. I pressed the on button.

The ship lit up, both inside and out, and the hatch automatically closed me in.

So, it would end like this, I realised to myself.

"Wait," cried a voice from the outside.

It was Nicolette, bathed in the light from the ship, waving at me in desperation.

I released the hatch and threw it back open.

"Take me with you," she pleaded. "We could be free together."

It only took me a second to process this.

"Sure we could," I replied, closing the hatch back over me, sending the ship up above the ground, and leaving Nicolette standing on the tarmac.

I pressed the accelerator and sent the ship forward, reaching for the sky.

EPILOGUE

ONCE A DUD

As the ship peeled away from the stadium, away from Dileag, I leaned back in my seat and breathed a sigh of relief, a sigh of freedom.

I clicked on the automatic pilot, put my hands behind my head and began to wonder:

Where would I go? What would I do? Who would I be?

None of that mattered.

All that mattered was that I would no longer be under the control of a...

"That was amazing," said a deeply accented voice from the back of the ship.

Queen Iyana, looking more magnificent than ever, appeared from the passenger area at the back of the craft and squeezed her glorious body into the co-pilot's seat, her long and luxurious hair falling down over her bare shoulders.

"At last we can be together," she said, casting me a knowing and seductive smile.

I quickly pressed the ejector button and sent Queen Iyana shooting into the air.

The hatch closed back over me.

I put my hands back behind my head, closed my eyes, and began to whistle...

ITEM 4: AFTERWORD – FRED BELLINGTON

This was the last of the pages labelled "A Dud's Tale."

I wonder what became of "Dud Wimpole."

Or I wonder what will become of him, perhaps I should say.

Either way, whoever uncovers the rest of the story, whoever tells the tale, it won't be me.

They don't allow books in the institution.

Fred Bellington
Former Primary School Teacher
30/11/2020

A Fairly Typical Relationship

Their relationship was fairly typical. They met when both in their late twenties, married in their early thirties. He was a teacher. She worked in an office. Harold and Polly.

A month after they were married, Polly sold her car for £2,500 pounds, and deposited the sum in Harold's savings account, which until then had been empty. She said she didn't really need the car, and quite fancied cycling to and from work each day.

A week later, Harold returned from work to find the house looking rather more spacious. The antique furniture Polly had brought with her when she moved in was gone, as was her extensive shoe collection, and most of the clothes from her wardrobe. For a moment, Harold was worried, but then Polly returned home waving a cheque in the air, saying: "I sold a load of shit on ebay today and earned you £10,000."

"What? How?" Harold asked, as Polly shoved the check into his hands.

"I took my annual leave day and just thought, do I really need this stuff? You can deposit that in your savings account."

Harold looked at the cheque in his hand. Ten thousand pounds.

"Well, at least let me take you out to dinner," he said.

"No, no, no," laughed Polly. "Why waste a load of money in a restaurant? Let's cook together. It'll be more fun! I'm just going to pop upstairs to see if there's any jewelry I can get rid of."

*

A week later, Harold was at home looking through some travel brochures. He'd deposited the £10,000 in his savings account, plus the £18,500 Polly had got for selling her jewelry. He was thinking about treating Polly and himself to a holiday, but Polly was an hour late returning from work and he was getting worried.

Then she suddenly burst through the door carrying a load of Aldi bags.

"They've opened a new discount food store down the other end of the motorway," cried Polly. "I've just saved £300 on our month's shopping and put the money in your savings account! If I keep this up we'll save £3,600 a year! That's £36,000 every ten years!"

"But how did you get it all home?" asked Harold.

"It was easy – on my handlebars. I evened out the bags so I was balanced! Ha ha!"

*

A few weeks later, Polly converted the front of their house into a take away food outlet.

"What are you doing?" asked Harold, as Polly, perched on a step ladder, hung a red and white canopy outside the front of their kitchen window.

"We always have so much food left over," said Polly. "With all the leftover ingredients I can make fruit shakes and barbeque kebabs and make a bit of extra money on the weekend. I'll stick it in your savings account."

"But why?" asked Harold.

Polly looked at him, puzzled. "For you," she explained, stepping down from the ladder. "You're my husband and I want you to be happy. I think freedom and choice are both key to happiness, and it's easier to have freedom and choice when you've got some money in your bank account, right?"

"Well, yeah, but I don't want you to strain yourself."

"I'm fine. I want to do it," said Polly. "And I want you to know that you can do whatever you like with any money I earn for you. You're free to indulge in all of your wishes and I won't judge, question or complain."

"Alright, then," said Harold. "Thanks."

A few weeks later, Polly took a second job working nights on railway maintenance. Her wages flooded into Harold's bank account and Harold and Polly got on fine.

And that's it, really; a fairly typical relationship.
True story.

Little Men

A Web-series in Six Handsome Parts

EPISODE 1: IN WHICH THE LITTLE MEN GET A LETTER FROM THEIR MOTHER, WHO IS AT WAR.

INT. MR. MARCH'S FLAT - DAY

JOE, ANDY, MEL and BEN, (30s/40), our LITTLE MEN, are crammed into their Dad's flat.

The flat is arranged to suit an elderly retiree, and not much more. Why the Little Men are still there, we do not know.

And why they are called Little, is yet to be determined. They may be little in stature, they may be little in prospects, they may be dwarfs.

Andy and Joe look out the window.

> ANDY
> It just so happens that
> a troupe of twenty-
> something
> international models
> live across the street.

> JOE
> Christine Columbus!

> MEL
> Joe! Don't use such
> dreadful expressions.

> ANDY
> (closing the
> curtain)
> They've spotted us!

> MEL
> Oh, bother. Now
> we'll be pestered to
> speak to them.

Dad (MR. MARCH) (70s) enters.

> MR. MARCH
> Glad to find you so
> merry, my boys.

> BEN
> Did you have a hard
> day, Dad?

> MR. MARCH
> No. Very pleasant,
> son. But it's good to
> be home. I have a
> treat for you.

Mr. March holds up a letter.

> BEN
> A letter from mother
> - from the front lines!

> MR. MARCH
> (reading)
> "Give them all my dear
> love and a kiss. Tell
> them I know they
> will remember all I said
> to them, that they will
> be loving sons to you,
> will do their duty
> faithfully, fight their
> bosom enemies bravely,
> and conquer themselves
> so beautifully, that
> when I come back to
> them from the war, I
> may be fonder and
> prouder than ever of
> my little men."

ANDY

I am a selfish man,
but I'll truly try to be
better and not waste
my time in school, so
that mother mayn't be
disappointed in me.

JOE

I'll try and be what
she loves to call me, 'a
little man', and not be
rough and wild; and
do my duty here at
home instead of
always wanting to go
to war to help
mother.

MEL

I'm not going to be
envious anymore, if I
can help it.

MR. MARCH

Now we'll save the
rest till after tea, for
it's such a lovely long
letter, and it must be
difficult to write when
up to your neck in
bullets at the race
wars. I know
everybody must be
hungry.

Mr. March exits to the kitchen.

                    BEN
        Let's get something
        for Dad with our
        Christmas money
        instead of for
        ourselves, shall we?

                    JOE
        That's like you, Ben.
        What shall we get?

                    MEL
        I shall get him a nice
        pair of gloves.

                    JOE
        New slippers! Best to
        be had!

                    BEN
        Some new
        handkerchiefs, all
        hemmed.

                    ANDY
        A beautiful little
        bottle of cologne.
        He'd like that and it
        won't cost much and
        then I'll have some
        left over for my
        pencils.

                    BEN
        We oughtn't spend
        money for pleasure,
        when our women are
        suffering so in the army.

Joe pulls back the curtains again.

                    JOE
I feel sorry for that
poor swim-suit model
who has to strut
around in a bikini all
day. Oh, look. There
she is!

                    ANDY
Where? Makes my
knees chatter just to
look at her.

                    MEL
Don't point, Joe.
She'll think you're
waving at her.

                    JOE
She's gone anyway.
Well, what if she
does? Hey? Hey?

Joe gets Mel into a head-lock.

                    MEL
    Joe!

The Little Men jump on each-other and wrestle on the floor,
laughing with great merriment and joy.

EPISODE 2: IN WHICH THE LITTLE MEN HAVE SAUSAGES FOR CHRISTMAS.

INT. MR MARCH'S FLAT - DAY

Church bells ring out, for it is Christmas.

Ben sits in an arm chair, reading the paper.

Joe enters.

>   JOE
> Merry Christmas,
> Ben.

>   BEN
> Oh, Merry Christmas.

>   JOE
> Where's Dad?

>   BEN
> He just went down
> the street. But he'll be
> right back. He
> wants us to have
> breakfast but I don't
> know how to make it.

Andy enters.

>   ANDY
> Don't laugh, Joe. I
> only changed the little
> bottle of cologne for
> a big one. I gave all of
> my money to get it. I
> felt ashamed thinking
> only of myself. And
> I'm so glad, because

mine's the
handsomest present
now. Where's Dad?

                    JOE
He'll be back any
minute. We're
wondering what to do
for breakfast!

                    ANDY
Oh, Joe. I'm so
hungry.

                    JOE
We all are. We're all
hungry.

Mel enters with a plate of sausages.

                    BEN
Oh, Mel, what is it?
Sausages!

                    MEL
Sausages. From the
neighbour - the
House of Models.
They said we look
hungry.

                    ANDY
Close the curtains!

                    JOE
Pigs in blankets!
Coffee! Oh! Mel,
you're some pumpkin!

MEL

You needn't make
such a fuss about it. I
can remember when I
used to put ketchup
on mother's sausages
every day. That was
my job.

ANDY

Oh, Mel. Were we
really that rich? I'd
like to imagine all the
stylish clothes I used
to wear.

JOE

I can imagine!
Diapers!

MEL

Joe!

JOE

Two each. Look at all
the onions.

MEL

Dad's coming!

JOE

Hurry up! Ben, get
forks and knives.
Andy, open the door.

Andy exits.

Come here, Mel. We'll
cover these up and
then it'll be a surprise.

Andy re-enters with Mr. March

LITTLE MEN

Merry Christmas,
Dad.

MR. MARCH

Merry Christmas. Oh
lads! Oh, Mel! Oh,
thank you. Oh, and
handkerchiefs from
Ben. Thank you. Oh,
Andy, my precious.
Cologne!

JOE

These are from me.

MR. MARCH

Oh, Joe. Joe, my son!
Gloves! Oh, thank
you. Thank you. Oh,
my little men. I can't
tell you how happy I
am.

JOE

Well, I can tell you
how hungry I am.
Come on, everyone.
Pass me those plates.
Dad, look! Sausages.

MR. MARCH

(suddenly
grave)
Wait a minute, sons. I
want to say one word
before we begin.
I've just come from a

poor man with a
newly adopted baby
and six adopted
children huddled into
one bed to keep from
freezing for they have
no fire, and he keeps
adopting children.
They're suffering cold
and hunger. Oh, my
sons, will you give
them your breakfast
as a Christmas
present?

                    JOE
Oh, for fuck's sake!

                    MR. MARCH
I knew you would.

                    JOE
              (furious
                 and
                 resentful)
I'm so glad you came
back before we
started.

                    ANDY
May I carry some
things, Dad?

                    MR. MARCH
We should all go.
Take the coffee, Mel.

                    BEN
I'll take some
firewood.

                    ANDY
I'll take the plate.

                    JOE
Takes the piss.

EPISODE 3: IN WHICH JOE INTRODUCES HIMSELF TO THE MODEL NEXT DOOR (SHE WHO SENT THE SAUSAGES).

EXT. HOUSE OF MODELS - DAY

Joe, holding a tray of blancmange, stands outside the neighbour's house, "The House of Models." He knocks on the door.

LAUREN, a stunning, six foot, 20 something model, opens.

> JOE
> How do you do? I
> wanted to thank you
> for the sausages.

Lauren sneezes onto the top of Joe's head... and polishes it clean.

> LAUREN
> Oh, excuse me. Just a
> little cold, but my
> manager's made me
> stop indoors for a
> week. Come in.

INT. HOUSE OF MODELS - DAY

Lauren leads Joe into the living room - a space decorated in large scale glamour photos of Lauren at European landmarks.

> JOE
> My brother, Mel, sent
> you some of his
> "blancmange". It's soft
> and will slide down
> your throat easily,
> without hurting. And,
> um, Ben lent you this.

Joe hands Lauren a small figurine of a footballer.

> LAUREN
>
> Thank you. I'm
> making tea.

Joe circles the room, looking at some of the wall-photos of
Lauren bending over fountains.

> JOE
>
> Christine Columbus!
> What a fountain! How
> do you like it here,
> after being in Europe,
> Miss...?

> LAUREN
>
> Lauren.

> JOE
>
> I'm going to Europe.

> LAUREN
>
> Really? When?

> JOE
>
> I don't know. You
> see, my Dad has
> rheumatism, and his
> doctor thought that
> the baths... Did you
> take any baths while
> you were there? I
> mean, for
> rheumatism.

> LAUREN
>
> No. No, I'm not
> troubled with
> rheumatism.

JOE

Nope. Neither am I.
I've always wanted to
go to Europe. Not for
the baths, of course.
But for my writing.
What were you saying,
Miss. Lauren?

LAUREN

I'm not Miss. Lauren.
I'm only Lauren.

JOE

Well, Lauren. Well,
how do you like it
here after Europe?

LAUREN

Well, it's strange after
living in studios all my
life. Oh, it'll
be alright when I get
used to my manager.
You know, she's...

JOE

Oh, yes! You should
have seen her before
you came. Whipping
some of the other
models...

LAUREN

Isn't she a holy terror?

Lauren hands Joe a dainty tea-cup.

JOE

Oh, it's too nice to

drink from. My
brother loves painting
china. He's very
artistic.

                    LAUREN
Andy?

                    JOE
Yes. How do you
know?

                    LAUREN
Why, I often hear you
calling to one another.
When I'm alone over
here, I beg your
pardon for being so
rude, but sometimes
you forget to put
down the curtain. It's
like looking at a
picture to see you all
around the TV with
your Dad. You always
seem to be having
such good times.

                    JOE
Perv as you please. I
wish, though, instead
of just peeping, you'd
come over and see us.
We'd have jolly times
together.

                    LAUREN
And would you let me
be in your play fights?
I saw you wrestling...

JOE

Oh, that was terrible.
Mel cheated. I want to
do karate, though.

LAUREN

I could do karate. I
took a lesson.

JOE

Really?

LAUREN

Yes! Look! Look!
Hiya!

Lauren throws a punch to mid-air.

JOE

Splendid!

LAUREN

Hiya.

Lauren throws another punch as Joe duck and dives around
her.

JOE

I strike you down,
Miyagi!

LAUREN

Hiya!

Lauren kicks Joe in the stomach.

He keels over.

JOE

A hit; what say you?

> LAUREN
> A touch. A touch. I
> do confess.

LISA (40s) enters, a glamorous woman in a power suit.

Joe remains keeled over, unable to stand. He extends his hand.

> LAUREN
> This is Lisa, my talent
> manager. Oh, I say.
> Oh, I say. You're
> hurt?

> JOE
> Oh, no. Nothing ever
> hurts me.

> LAUREN
> I'm sorry. I forgot
> you're only a little
> man, and I'm afraid I
> got a bit too rough.

> JOE
> Oh, what are you
> talking about? Oh, I
> had you bettered, if I
> hadn't slipped. Oh,
> that's a good picture
> of you in Paris.

> LISA
> Shall I call an
> ambulance?

> JOE
> I must be going.

Joe edges to the door.

> ### LAUREN
> There's a party here,
> tomorrow. You'll
> come, won't you?
> And your brothers?

> ### JOE
> Absolutely. I'll be
> fully recovered by
> then.

Lauren holds the door open for Joe as he leaves.

> ### JOE
> Cheers. Bye

Lauren watches the Little Man go.

EPISODE 4: IN WHICH THE LITTLE MEN GET READY FOR AND GO TO A PARTY.

INT. MR. MARCH'S FLAT - DAY

Mr. March sits alone, reading the newspaper.

The Little Men enter, Joe, Andy, Mel and Ben, well groomed.

> MR. MARCH
> Here they come. Here
> they come. All
> dressed up and
> looking handsome.

> BEN
> Oh, Dad, I wish
> Lauren hadn't asked
> us to her party. I'm
> frightened.

> MR. MARCH
> You wouldn't want to
> hurt her feelings when
> she's been so kind.
> Oh, Joe, you look
> splendid.

> JOE
> Well, I feel perfectly
> miserable with 19
> bottles of hair-gel all
> sticking straight into
> my head.

> MR. MARCH
> Does the patch show
> much?

Joe turns to reveal a home-made patch covering his ass.

                    MEL
It does a little, Dad.
But he's going to sit
down or stand
with his back against
the wall. Joe, where
are your gloves?

                    JOE
Oh, well, I've stained
them so I'm gonna go
without.

                    MEL
You wear gloves, or I
don't go.

                    ANDY
I tried to clean them
but it only made them
look worse.

Andy holds up a pair of dirty gloves.

                    JOE
Oh, here. I'll carry
them. I'll hold them
crumpled up in one
hand. Nobody'll see
them.

                    MEL
All right. And do
behave nicely and
don't put your hands
behind your back.
Good night, Dad.

> MR. MARCH
> Have a nice time.
> Remember, the
> sooner you're all
> married, the sooner
> I'm a free man, so
> play it cool, put on
> the charm.

INT. HOUSE OF MODELS - DAY

Andy dances in the centre of the living room.

Joe stands with his back to wall.

Ben and Mel stand awkwardly by a table with drinks.

Manageress Lisa approaches.

> LISA
> What's this? Why
> aren't you two little
> men dancing?

> MEL
> Dad said we were to
> play it cool, to turn on
> the charm.

> LISA
> (to Ben)
> Perhaps you would
> like to choose the
> music.

> MEL
> He just likes to listen
> to the music.

                    LISA

You help yourself to
the laptop. Be the DJ.

                    BEN

Oh, no. No, mam.
Please.

                    LISA

Why not? Well, my
dear boy, what's the
matter?

                    MEL

He has an infirmity.

                    LISA

Mmm?

                    MEL

He's shy.

                    LISA

Oh, I see.

                    MEL

If it weren't for that,
he'd be simply
fastidious because he
DJs beautifully.

                    LISA

Oh, he must come
and play for me
sometime.

                    MEL

No. He never would.

LISA

Oh, it wasn't that I
wanted to hear him,
but that DJ software
is simply going to ruin
for want of use. I was
hoping one of you
little men would come
and practice on it. Just
to keep it in tune, you
know. Well, if you
don't care to come,
never mind.

BEN

Oh, mam. We do
care, very, very much.

LISA

So you're the musical
one.

BEN

I'm Ben. I love it
dearly and I'll do it if
you're quite sure no-
one will hear me and
be disturbed.

LISA

Not a soul, my little
man. Not a soul. You
come too, young
chap. And tell your
father I think all his
sons are simply
"fastidious".

Ben moves over to a lap-top and shifts the tempo of the
music, prompting Andy to dance wildly.

Lauren approaches Joe, who remains fixed against the wall.

LAUREN
Don't you like to dance?

JOE
Oh, yes. I love to
dance, but I can't. I
mean, I promised I
wouldn't.

LAUREN
Why?

JOE
Oh, well, I may as
well tell you. You
won't tell?

LAUREN
Silence to the death.

JOE
Well, you see, I have a
bad trick of standing
in front of the
fire and I scorch my
jeans, and I burned
this pair.

LAUREN
Where?

Joe shows Lauren his patched butt-cheek.

JOE
Oh, you can laugh if
you want to. It is
funny.

                    LAUREN
          There's no one in the
          toilet. We can dance
          in there without being
          seen.

                     JOE
          You're a champ!

INT. HOUSE OF MODELS - TOILET - DAY

Lauren spins Joe around in the toilet.

                    LAUREN
          This is regularly
          splendid.

                     JOE
          Cheers.

EPISODE 5: IN WHICH SLIPPERS ARE PRESENTED.

INT. HOUSE OF MODELS - HALLWAY NIGHT

Lauren holds the door open for The Little Men as they leave the party.

> THE LITTLE MEN
> Good night. Night.
> Thank you.

Mel stops and faces Lisa in the hallway.

> MEL
> These... these are for
> you.

Mel hands Lisa some slippers.

> LISA
> Slippers?

> MEL
> When Lauren makes
> it big, and leaves,
> what becomes of you?

> LISA
> I shall turn soldier as
> soon as she is off. I'm
> needed.

> MEL
> I'm sorry. I mean, I'm
> so sorry for all the
> fathers and brothers
> who have to stay
> home and worry.

> LISA

Yes, it must be
difficult for them.
Luckily, I have
neither. And few
friends to care if I live
or die.

> MEL

Lauren would care a
great deal. And we...
we all would be very
sorry if any harm
came to you.

> LISA

Would you?

Joe peers his head back in the door.

> JOE

Thanks for inviting
us! Cheers!

> LISA

It's been a most
enjoyable evening.

> MEL

Thank you. Paying
visits has never been
quite so much fun
before.

> LISA

I hope we may do it
again, very soon.

JOE
Good-bye, Miss. Lisa.
Come along, Mel.

LISA
Good-bye, Little Mel.

MEL
Good-bye.

LAUREN
Good-bye, Joe. See
you tomorrow, Joe -
for our walk.

Lauren closes the door.

INT. MR. MARCH'S FLAT - NIGHT

Mel paces the room in front of the fellow Little Men.

MEL
I've never been so
embarrassed in my
life. When will you
stop your childish
romping ways?

JOE
Not until I'm old and
stiff and have to use a
crutch.

Mr. March enters holding an envelope.

MR. MARCH
This has just been
posted through the
door. I'll read it.
"Little Mel. Dear sir."

ANDY

Isn't that elegant?

MR. MARCH
(reading)
"I've had many pairs
of slippers in my life,
but none has suited
me as well as yours. I
like to pay my debts,
so I know you will
allow me to send you
something that
belonged to the little
father I lost. Your
Lisa." Oh, Mel! It
opens. It opens.

Mr. March holds up a silver locket.

BEN

Isn't it romantic?

JOE

Romantic? Rubbish!
I've never heard of
anything so horrid.
Trying to break up
other people's
happiness and spoil
all their fun!

ANDY

It doesn't spoil any
fun! Makes it twice as
good! You'll find out
when someone falls in
love with you. Your
lover's arms around
you...

154

JOE

I'd like to see anybody
try it.

ANDY

Would you? Oh!.....
I'll get you…... Now
I've got you…..

Andy chases Joe and gets him in a headlock.

JOE

Why can't we stay as
we are? Do you have
to go and fall in love,
and spoil all our
peace, and fun and
happy times together?
Don't go and marry
that woman.

MEL

If you mean Lisa, she
hasn't asked me. But
if she should, I shall
merely say, quite
calmly and decidedly,
"I'm sorry, but I agree
with father that it's
too soon."

MR. MARCH

Hang on a minute...

JOE

Oh, Mel. Hoorah for
you. Hoorah!

The Little Men wrestle on the floor as Mr. March looks on in
dismay.

EPISODE 6: IN WHICH LAUREN DECLARES HER
LOVE FOR JOE.

EXT. CLIFF-TOPS - DAY

The wind sweeps over the Cliftonville cliff-tops.

Joe and Lauren walk side by side.

> LAUREN
> Lisa enlisted in the
> army so suddenly. She
> goes to the front lines
> tomorrow.

> JOE
> I hope Mel rejecting
> her like that had
> nothing to do with it.

> LAUREN
> I'll be ok, I guess, by
> myself.

> JOE
> You don't have to
> stay here.

> LAUREN
> Why? Should we run
> off and join a pirate
> ship?

Lauren looks at Joe and inhales, about to talk.

Joe sees her face and immediately knows what is about to
happen.

JOE
(panicking)
No, Lauren, don't.

LAUREN
It's no use, Joe. We've
got to have it out.

JOE
No, no, we don't...

LAUREN
I've loved you ever
since I've known you,
Joe. I couldn't help it,
and you've been so
good to me. I've tried
to show it but you
wouldn't let me; now
I'm going to make
you hear and give me
an answer because I
can't go on like this
any longer.

JOE
I thought you'd
understand...

LAUREN
(not listening to him)
I've worked hard to
please you, and I gave
up billiards and
everything you didn't
like, and waited and
never complained for
I hoped you'd love
me, though I'm not
half good enough...

JOE

Yes, you are, you're a
great deal too good
for me, and I'm so
grateful to you and so
proud of you, I don't
see why I... I can't
love you as you want
me to.

LAUREN

You can't?

JOE

(helplessly)
I can't change the
feeling and it would
be a lie to say I do
when I don't. I'm so
sorry, Lauren, so
desperately sorry, but
I can't help it...

Lauren backs away from Joe, in pain.

LAUREN

I can't love anyone
else.

JOE

It would be a disaster
if we married, we'd be
miserable! I need the
space to write, the
time...

LAUREN

If you loved me Joe, I
would give you that
space!

            JOE
I can't - I've tried it
and failed.

            LAUREN
Everyone expects it -
your Dad and your
brothers. Joe, say you
will and let's be
happy!

            JOE
I can't say "Yes" truly
so I won't say it at all.

Lauren breaks down in tears.

            JOE
You'll see that I'm
right, eventually, and
you'll thank me for it.

            LAUREN
I'll be hanged if I do!

            JOE
You'll find some lovely
accomplished man, who
will adore you, and make
a fine husband for your
fine house. I wouldn't.
I'd hate elegant society
and you'd hate my
scribbling, and I'd lose
my looks, and my body,
and we would be
unhappy and wish we
hadn't done it and
everything will be horrid.

                    LAUREN
Anything more?

                    JOE
Nothing more -
except that...
          (honest)
I don't believe I will
ever marry. I'm happy
as I am, and love my
liberty too well to be
in any hurry to give it
up.

                    LAUREN
          (shaking
            her
            head)
You will care for
somebody, and you'll
love her
tremendously, and
live and die for her. I
know you will, it's
your way, and you will
and I'll watch.

Lauren runs away.

Joe turns to face the sea.

                    JOE
Men have minds and
souls as well as hearts,
ambition and talent as
well as beauty and I'm
sick of being told that
love is all a little man
is fit for. But... I am
so lonely.

THE END

Printed in Great Britain
by Amazon

58299723R00102